Tanked

By Leslie Butt

Publisher: Leslie Butt

Cover Art: Krystahh Lawlor

Cover Photo: Krystahh Lawlor

ISBN: 978-0-9781150-3-6
ISBN-EPUB: 978-0-9781150-2-9

1

I was born from stars that have forgotten to shine
The universe will show me where I will align
To create my destiny, even though I bleed
To realize that I am all that I need

I grew up in a small town, which was difficult for someone like me. I lived in the kind of town where everyone knows who you are, good or bad. I would walk down hallways and hear people whispering about me and my family. No matter where I went, people knew my name. It was reciprocal, as well. The same people had worked at the gas station and the corner store for as long as I could remember. The same neighbours. The monotony may have been the worst part of it all, and I craved adventure and escape, no matter how I had to make it happen.

There wasn't much to do in the place where I spent my teenage years. There was the option of going to the coffee shop, where the coffee was brewed so strong and tart that it was impossible to drink without sugar; and where the plastic ferns on the window ledges spilled over the edges like spider legs. You could sit down in a fast-food restaurant for a three-dollar burger and fries, the grease bleeding into the parchment packaging while turning your hands slick. You could run across the road to buy something at the drugstore—a cheap chocolate bar and a dollar eyeshadow. Otherwise, if you weren't an outdoor person who owned a horse, a dirt bike, or a good tent, you were shit out of luck.

There was one other option if you were sick of the terrible coffee at the coffee shop, or your parents never bought you expensive outdoor sports accessories—drink, smoke weed, and party. I found myself falling into that last category.

There was an old railroad track that spanned the entire length of the town. It started near the river and went for miles through the woods. My favourite place was the part of "The Tracks", as we called them, on top of the bridge near the river. You could look down and see the raging water and waterfalls from either side. Most people used The Tracks to

1

party, or to ride snowmobiles once the snow fell. The area had been deemed a National Historic Site because it used to be an old glacier.

The glacier had carved out a canyon, which filled with pools of water where people would swim during the summer. There was also a rock formation that people used as a waterslide. I could see the canyon from the window of my classroom, and there was something placid about the water. I would spend a lot of time at that river—watching, writing, drawing, and looking for fossils, which I liked to collect. It was easier to think of what used to exist than to think about my current situation.

I had the sense my parents never did want children at all. My dad basically ignored me, and spent most of his time partying in the basement. My mom had given up on us years ago, choosing a party life herself. I hadn't talked to her in five years. All the same, I still checked the mail and waited by the phone every day.

I was lucky to have her brother, who lived on the other side of the country. He called me every Sunday. Sometimes he would send me little trinkets in the mail—calligraphy pens, CDs, books about fossils. Without that to look forward to I probably would have lost my mind.

It was even harder to find friends who cherished things like books or philosophy. I was lucky to have a couple of friends that cared for me, although their lives were a lot more conventional than mine. I tried my best to conceal my reality from them, and they were happy to have me around, even though I'd often disappear to play guitar or write a poem.

Sometimes I wished that I could have been the type of person that could just have a good time without assessing every detail of a situation, and plummeting into an abyss of anxiety. Nothing erases the years I was just painfully different. I spent most of my time alone.

My room was small, but it was my sanctuary. Despite the disrepair of our house, I managed to decorate my room with paper swans. I made them from paper I'd stolen from the art room at school; and I hung patchwork curtains made from old clothing my friend Jessica had given me. Her mom would buy her a whole new wardrobe every school year, and I was fortunate to get her hand-me-downs. Before those curtains, the plastic blinds were tattered and torn, and I would not even raise them up to let the light in.

Although my bed took up most of the room, I had a little side table where I kept my paper and pens, and a drawer for my vodka and cigarettes. I nailed blankets to the walls in an attempt to insulate the room from the sounds and smells of my dad and his friends in the basement. Sometimes he would forget to pay the heat bill so the blankets also did a good job of keeping some heat in the room, especially if I had to turn on a space heater. If there was no power, I would use candles to heat the room. I learned to get boiling water in a thermos at the coffee shop and put it under my blankets in bed. At least the hot water was free.

When I couldn't bear to be home any longer, I would walk The Tracks with my paper and pen. Sometimes, I would sit in the middle of the woods, wonder about my future, and write poems and songs about how I yearned to leave this town.

I will set alight
With the fires that burn in my mind
As I scatter these seeds
Of these flames of my dreams
I make this wish and
I am one with the breeze

Our house was this dilapidated little bungalow on the corner of the main road, about two blocks from my school, Sacred Heart High. The wood on the bottom of the house was visibly rotting and falling off, and the steps to get to the front door were missing a few boards. I avoided inviting anyone over. It was embarrassing that my house was so different from the other two-story houses next to it, the ones with nice siding.

Sometimes school was an oasis, as I could get a free lunch, fill up my water bottle, and warm up. I didn't mind the school work. I had a passion for learning, and I loved working my way through the school library. Other times it was pure torture.

"Good morning, Lily," my favourite teacher, Mr. Crowley, said one morning, gesturing me to his direction. He held out a little black notebook and a sandwich in a Ziplock bag.

"These are for you. Have a nice day now, okay?"

I was quiet and had good grades. I was often absent because there were other girls in the school who would push me into lockers and call me poor as I walked by. They had even resorted to stealing my poems and taping them to the walls, which was embarrassing.

One day I was called out of class by the Vice Principal, Mrs. Hodder. It wasn't a regular occurrence for me to get into trouble, so I became concerned.

"Lily, you can confess now and we can figure out a suitable punishment, but I can guarantee you that we do not tolerate lying or vandalism at this school." She lowered her eyes as if I were a specimen in a petri dish.

"Pardon me, Miss, I am not sure what you mean."

She clicked her tongue and turned on her heels quickly.

"Come with me."

I obliged, and she led me to the girl's washroom. I was still as perplexed as I had been moments before. She gestured for me to go in. I reluctantly entered the washroom. The entirety of a bathroom stall had been marked up with permanent marker and pen. Based on the different types of writing, it was clear there were multiple people involved.

"Lily is a fat ugly whore."

"Lily should kill herself."

"Lily is a slut that looks like someone kicked her with a boot."

3

"The world would be better off if Lily was dead."

"Lily is too poor to even pay attention."

It took me about twenty minutes to read it all. If I'd had any tears left, I probably would have cried. One graffiti martyr decided to defend me, which ultimately became my downfall.

"Now, it is obvious this was you defending yourself, and probably you wrote this in the first place. Please go home. You are suspended for a week."

This was before I'd learned to fight and the injustice of it all rendered me speechless. There never was an investigation into who wrote it.

Some days it was hard to have motivation, so I would stay home and drink my vodka and write music instead. It was a delicate balance between wanting to be around people and wanting to be alone.

The summer I was fifteen, I was sitting behind the drugstore on a sunny afternoon. I was minding my own business, smoking a cigarette and sketching the dismal way the trees looked against the telephone poles. The sky was foggy and overcast, and despite the heat, everything seemed cold and depressing.

I worked at an ice cream shop down the street. It was open for the summer season only. I truly needed the money, and work was necessary for my sanity, but it was my day off. I dreaded my days off. I was sick of being alone, and Jessica was working at the coffee shop. I couldn't stand one more second trapped in my room, so I walked The Tracks to come out behind the gas station. There was a little perch in one of the shipping bays where no one could see me. I was wishing something would come along and save me from that treacherous day, when I looked up and he was standing there.

"Hey, can you sell me a smoke?" His eyes peered at me from under his trendy hat.

"You can just have one." I took my smokes from my pocket.

"So, do you live around here?" he asked, eyeing up my tanned arms. I was wearing the black t-shirt Jessica had given me.

"I don't know how much living anyone does around here, but yes."

He chuckled, as he took a drag of the cigarette and tapped his ash. The smoke blew from his mouth into my direction.

"What about you?" I asked, taking a drag from my own cigarette. I had gotten too far to the bottom of the smoke, and singed my pointer finger enough to flinch slightly. I threw the butt on the ground.

"I am staying with my aunt up the street. I just joined the army but I am staying here until I get my training call because the airport is closer here. Plus, I was getting bored at home, my girlfriend dumped me and I had to get out of there. Whatever, fuck her."

"Sorry to hear that. You're probably not going to find a girlfriend any better in this town, either."

"Are you single?"

I was taken aback by his question, since we had just met.

"I am not interested, but I like friends."

"Fair enough," he said, "don't mind me, I have just been lonely."

He looked down at his feet, and seemed briefly sad. He kicked his foot into the ground, like a child who was just told they couldn't have another cookie. Though it was an awkward minute, I felt some sympathy for him, and he was being respectful enough that I was fine with continuing the exchange.

We sat down and smoked together and talked. His hometown was an equally shitty small town a few hours away. He made me laugh, and our conversation wasn't at all forced.

"So, I was thinking we could head to a bar and have a few beers," he asked.

"Actually, I am only eighteen," I lied

"I can pick up a case, if you know somewhere we can go to drink it."

Chris picked up a dozen beers and I brought him from The Tracks to the woods, about a mile away from the river. We drank and kept talking. The beer was getting warm in the heat, despite us having laid it in a shadow under a tree. We had found a couple of tree stumps to perch on, far enough off the trail that no one could see if they walked by. There was no clear path, but I had been here before, as I was always exploring new spots to write.

The beer was the light kind. I would have bought something a little stronger, but the warmth brought out the taste of the barley, enough that it seemed stronger than it really was. He had about five beers, and I was on my third, when the greyness started to lift a little. The cigarettes gave just enough of a head-spin to cause a minute of a high.

We started to get goofy and laugh at nothing. I was so grateful to be taken out of the boring day, and I loved the adventure of not knowing what was going to happen next. We were back and forth telling jokes, and by the time I had my fourth beer, you couldn't wipe the smile off my face. I was having carefree fun. I was able to forget what was waiting for me at home. Or what was not waiting for me.

And then, it was like a shift in the sky, of his energy, and I realized there was a different kind of look in his eyes. He was looking at me as if I was a piece of meat. The day turned back into being grey and cold, and I looked around for the easiest way to leave quickly.

"So, do you want to have some fun?" he slurred. Both of us were pretty drunk now.

"What kind of fun were you thinking?" I asked. I wasn't dumb, and I could play along.

He didn't give me a chance to reply before unzipping his pants.

"I know you want me."

It hit me like a ton of bricks, what it was going to be like to be a woman. To always watch your back, because every man could think you want them without any prior indication. To always have to take a deep breath, to always walk on eggshells, and to be told the things you were doing were wrong.

I was shocked into silence. It felt as if I were above my body and looking down, and I found myself fighting off his slobbery lips, his hands on my back.

Luckily, he was drunk and tripped up in a tree stump. He landed on the ground, too drunk to get back up. I was drunk too, but he drank a lot faster than I did and was, for sure, more sloshed. I stumbled into an upright position and ran out of the woods, anticipating him running behind me. My heart was pounding, sweat pouring from my forehead, but somehow, I still felt cold. I felt like I was no longer in my own body, unsure of how I kept running. Once I made it back to The Tracks, I jogged towards the river, closer to home.

I made it through my door around supper time, and I locked it behind me. I spent the night jumping at every sound and looking out the window to make sure he hadn't followed me. The morning light finally came, and I hoped he would not see me working at the ice cream shop later that day.

2

A few weeks passed. Chris had gone off to the army, so I felt like I could finally breathe again. The hot July sun burned my skin as I walked through town with my notebook. My father was sleeping in until the early hours of the evening and we rarely crossed paths. I could hear the clang of beer bottles in the middle of the night, though, as wisps of cigarette smoke lingered in the air.

I got myself ready for work. The uniform was a grey shirt with the ice cream store logo, a hairnet and ugly matching hat, for which my manager took thirty dollars out of my cheque. I made $5.25 per hour, roughly the cost of a pack of cigarettes. When I worked a long shift, I would repeat the mantra, "One hour for one pack," and it amused me enough to keep me going.

We were not allowed to have breaks, so I chain smoked on my way to the store. It was on the main road, just past the river. It was an ugly pink building with a toddler-quality mural of ice cream cones painted on the side. If we worked longer than eight hours, the manager bought a pizza and we were allowed to quickly scarf down a slice in the back room.

Most people that worked there were teenagers, likely because teenagers weren't aware of employment laws. The couple of employees that were older than seventeen were related to the owner, which meant they had an inflated sense of authority. Luckily, the lineup was always out the door and around the back, so I was busy enough that I didn't have to interact with them much.

I made my way around the customers in the lineup, and entered through a little employee gate at the end of the coolers. This led behind the tubs of ice cream and sneeze guards, where I could start serving.

"Hey, Lily!"

"Hey Chad, busy day?"

"Well, let's just say we are earning our money fairly today," he responded, laughing.

He was always upbeat, so I tried to match his mood whenever we worked together. He was in the same grade as me at school, but had a pretty normal life. I made sure no one knew how I lived, even though I was sure there were rumours.

"Get to work, Lily," scolded Allison, the teenaged niece of the owner, her mouth in the usual straight line.

"Of course, boss," I replied, with a hint of undetectable sarcasm.

I was a hard worker, and enjoyed serving customers. It was a little bit like acting—I could pretend to be someone else for a while. I aimed to please, even though I would age out of this career path in a couple of years. I especially loved seeing the smiling children enjoying their treats, even if it made me slightly envious. With so much to do at work, the hours passed quickly, which brought me closer to having to go home.

"Chad!" Allison yelled from across the coolers, as I was standing in between them. "Come get this roll of pennies for your till."

"I can bring it over," I offered, taking a step towards her.

"No, HE has to bring it, because it is for his cash, not yours," she exclaimed, looking at me as if I had suggested we set the building on fire.

"Okay." I retreated, briefly irritated for being treated like some sort of thief.

As day turned into evening, I scarfed down a slice of cold pizza. Allison was in the back room counting our tills, and Chad and I finally got some reprieve from her attitude. We cleaned up the store.

"So, school next month, what are you taking?" Chad asked.

"I was looking forward to that oil painting class," I said. Oil paint was a far cry from the dried-up dollar store acrylics that I could afford.

"Nice, are you going to art school after grad?"

I smiled, because it would have been nice to have money to go to art school. Knowing it was so inaccessible seemed like a cruel joke. It was endearing to think that Chad didn't realize what my home life was like. I was lucky to eat.

"We will see," I replied.

"Lily!" Allison yelled, storming from the back room. "Somebody stepped on a cherry and you need to scrape it off the floor. Now."

"Yes, boss," I said, making my way over to the cherry. I looked up at Chad and rolled my eyes. He smiled and shook his head.

"Would you like a ride home?" Chad asked, after we had finished cleaning up. It was astounding how many teenagers had brand new cars. I barely had water to take a shower.

"I actually enjoy my walk home, but thanks."

I would have loved to get into that fancy car, but I didn't want Chad to see my shitty house. He might not talk to me ever again. We said our goodbyes and made our way to very different houses. We would do it all again tomorrow.

As summer dragged on, I spent my time working or wandering around town with the hot sun blaring down my back. Sometimes, I would sit and just watch the gorgeous man with the long hair who worked at the sub shop; the blonde bartender smoking out the backdoor of the shipping bay where I met Chris; the old man who sat at the coffee shop staring into space for hours.

As I made my way through the books at the library, I became engrossed in philosophy, reading through large texts in a matter of hours. I started with classics such as Plato and Aristotle, and then I moved on to the more postmodern works that I preferred, such as Foucault and Nietzsche. I sat at the coffee shop and sketched. I found beauty in the ugliness around me—the colour of burning cigarette embers in the darkness of lonely nights; the way the light hit Jessica's head like a halo while she slung coffees; the one dandelion floating at the top of the raging river. How I wished it would make it to the end safely.

During the lonely nights, I'd take vodka from my dad's liquor cabinet. I refilled the bottle with water so he wouldn't notice. I was certain he wouldn't anyway, it was just to save face and avoid having to pay him back. I would scavenge the ashtrays for roaches, like the street kids that sometimes panhandled outside the coffee shop on their way to hitchhiking to the city. They were much braver than I, because they knew they had to leave; but they had each other, while I was still alone.

My guitar was a five-dollar yard sale find. There was a man we called Doc who owned a guitar repair shop by the school, and he changed my strings for free whenever I needed them. I had a sense he knew what my life was like. I'd pick up my guitar and sing breathy vocals into the warm night.

I am a very hard person to love
The Kind you should run away from
I will leave stains on your heart
Like pools of black ink are draining from my scars
It will splatter onto my page again
Showing where my pain begins

I stopped caring for company, decided it wasn't worth it, thought of myself as the only person I needed. I realized that being alone was my only option.

At another day of work, while doing my best to avoid Allison, a customer entered. I had often seen him around town with his group of friends. He was probably about twenty, wearing a dress shirt that didn't quite match his face, and I could feel his gaze burning into me. As I was wiping ice cream remnants from a counter, he approached me.

"Hey," he said awkwardly, "my name is Colin."

He put out his hand, so I wiped off the ice cream in my uniform before shaking it.

"My name is Lily. Good to meet you."

We shared a couple of mundane sentences, how about this weather we're having, seen any good movies lately? After a couple of minutes,

Allison saw me and shot daggers through her eyes from the office window. It was not productive to talk to customers for too long. Colin got the hint to wrap up the dull chit-chat.

"Maybe we can hang out sometime?"

"Sure," I replied, handing him my phone number on the back of a neglected receipt.

I went home to a musty, smoke filled house. I lit up joints and cigarettes, played guitar chords until the world seemed to make sense. I was too tired to muster up the energy to come up with lyrics. I just wanted to forget.

It was the kind of summer where the days seemed to meld together and if you had nothing to do it wasn't hard to forget about linear time. I was in my own head, the days and nights didn't matter, an hour felt like months, and weeks seemed like seconds. The sweat rolled off my back in the sunny days and I spent the evenings alone, working on creative projects while getting fucked up by myself. If I wasn't working, I was thinking, drinking, drawing.

I developed a taste for beer. The smooth coolness down my throat gave me energy, as opposed to the burning vodka that put me to sleep. I drew Colin's anxious gaze, how one side of his dress shirt was untucked, Allison glaring at us in the background with an irritated frown.

It was at least a week before I heard from Colin. We made plans to meet up a few days later at the river. It was pretty much the only thing the town was proud of.

The long days of summer brought many tourists to view what was regarded as a natural wonder. Luckily, the travellers never stayed long enough to see me walking the roads by myself, lugging home heavy bags of books from the library, the smoke escaping from lips stained with red wine. These observations were saved for the old man in the coffee shop, the bartender, the sub guy. Though I saw these people so often it was as if they were friends to me, we had never actually been introduced. Seeing them all gave me a sense of comfort and normalcy.

We met up at the river. It was a beautiful day. We headed to the ice cream shop, at his suggestion. I was allowed to get things from the ice cream store on my "tab", which would be taken out of my pay. This was fortunate since I had spent all my money on beer and cigarettes. I was hoping Allison was hiding in her office.

"So," he said gingerly, "you must eat a lot of ice cream working here. I would!"

"Mostly pizza actually, which is a long story," I said, as we inched through the lineup.

When we got to the counter, Chad took our order. Colin ordered a banana split, jumbo, so presumably we could share. I wasn't a huge fan of bananas, or even ice cream actually, but since he wordlessly paid, I wasn't going to complain about free food. He thanked Chad, which made me appreciate him more. Many customers were thankless.

We headed outside to the back of the store where there was a collection of picnic benches scattered around the grass. He sat next to me, instead of across, and I could feel his nervousness. There was something else there, too. It was an air of confidence he possessed, of never having been broken, of knowing what to say and do without overthinking. He handed me a spoon.

"So," he said between bites of ice cream, wiping his face with his sleeve mid-sentence, "what do you want to be when you grow up?"

"Well, definitely not an ice cream man," I joked, as much as I hated talking about the future. I was just trying to survive the present.

He laughed.

"You're pretty funny for a chick. In September I am starting a science degree. Not really what I want to do but my mom is making me, which is super annoying. I wanted to take a couple years off to travel, but she wouldn't give me my trust fund if I didn't go. So, it will have to be between semesters now, which blows."

"Ugh, that's just the worst," I replied, pretending to know the feeling.

"Well, what else do you like to do?"

"My parents live on a lake and I love going on the Seadoo, it's totally awesome." He wiped his mouth with his sleeve again, and ran his hand through his hair. "But yeah, I really don't want to get a job until the fall so I can enjoy the summer. Must be a bummer to work, are your parents making you buy your own car or something?"

"Oh totally, they spent my car fund on the pool and hot tub," I joked sarcastically.

"Total bummer," he replied seriously. "At least you don't have to swim in the river!"

The evening brought a cool breeze and he wrapped me in his arms to keep me warm. I had forgotten a sweater that day. He was so large and warm; he was a real man. His arms around me made me feel safe. The way his hand rubbed my upper arm, the faint smell of cologne, the setting sun, all made me smile. I finally had a friend; someone to call, someone to hang out with, someone to think of.

When the sun set, he called a few friends. One of them picked us up in their new car, a present from mom, I surmised. We went back to Colin's place, and I got along extremely well with his friends. It was the first time I had found people I could almost see as being my own friends. We sipped whiskey from a stainless-steel flask, and played guitar. We had a fire in the backyard and smoked a joint. I wished the night would never end, knew that later it would just be me at home, entertaining myself and washing the dishes. Inevitably, the time came to leave, and this is when Colin first kissed me.

I wasn't sure what was supposed to happen next, he said he would call me. Lying in bed that night, high on marijuana and human contact, I sure hoped he would. I thought of how lucky people were to have friends, to have their calendars filled with plans, to have people doting on them. But maybe happiness was dangerous. It made you think of all the things that made you unhappy. I fell asleep on top of the covers hoping he would call.

And he did, the next day. We made plans to meet up at his place later that afternoon. I wasn't the type of person that spent too much time on my appearance. I didn't buy makeup or the newest clothes. I was happier in skirts I bought for a dollar. I liked putting colours together, it was the artist in me. I'd rather have spent my money on someone else or good food than to waste it on attracting the wrong kinds of people. However, that day, I found myself in front of a mirror in my best black lace top, curling my hair with my mom's old eighties curling iron, and tearing the bathroom apart for some lipstick.

For someone so messed up in the head, Mom always looked gorgeous. Her flowing black hair curled neatly, red lipstick, fancy shoes, the smell of her leather purse, and the minty smell inside from her pack of gum. I always wished I could know how to be as beautiful, but my hair and makeup were rarely complete.

He picked me up around noon, gave me a lingering hug as I sat down into the passenger seat.

"You look really nice," he uttered into my neck before he pulled away and started driving.

"Thanks, you as well."

Men never really made me nervous, but I found that around Colin I wasn't sure what to do with my hands. I had to think about what I was going to say before I said it, and there was an awkward formality to us being together.

At least he wasn't another Chris. He was a nice guy, wearing a collared shirt, on the fast track to a large salary career in medicine. He may not have been the most interesting person in the world, but he knew how to treat me. He opened doors, asked me if I was cold, cooked me food at his house.

His house was impressive. He lived with his parents, but it seemed very worth it. I guess if you have a somewhat functional family it isn't as if every day is a battle in sanity. The house was on the outskirts of town and built right onto a lake. It even had a boathouse. All the walls and floors seemed brand new and everything was decorated like a cable TV home makeover show. I even recognized some of the paintings on the walls.

He had the whole basement to himself, a full apartment, short of a kitchen. We hung out on the couch and absent-mindedly watched a movie, while discussing whatever came to our minds. We sat there pretty much the whole day, basking in each other's energy and warmth.

"So," he asked after one of the movies ended, "What do you think is going to happen when you die?" He draped his arm around my neck. "Do you believe in heaven, or hell, or is it all just a fabrication of society so we don't go insane?"

"I'm not sure yet, I haven't thought about it enough to really decide. What do you believe in?"

"I think that there is something bigger than us but I haven't really deciphered what it is yet. I do believe in love, though, man. Just, love everyone, you know, everyone deserves to be loved, and everyone should have sex with each other, it should just be an open society."

His last comment made me cold inside

"Can I ask you a question," he said slyly, narrowing his eyes.

"Sure." That couldn't have been more opposite a statement. I was uncomfortable and wanted more than anything to leave.

"Have you ever just held a penis?"

I may have been fifteen, but I wasn't stupid. I took my cue, and stood up and gathered my things.

"Where are you going? Why are you being dramatic?"

"Hell," I said, as I opened the door, "because that's what I believe in."

3

I tried to pick up as many shifts as possible at the ice cream store. On the first of the month, I left four hundred dollars on the kitchen counter for my dad, as per our agreement. Whatever was left over I wasted away on any alcohol and cigarettes I could get my hands on. Getting alcohol and drugs at fifteen was surprisingly easy. I smoked a pack of cigarettes a day and blew the rest on coffee and vintage clothes from the thrift store. When I wasn't working, I was drunk, high or wandering the streets by myself.

For weeks, I barely spoke, fearing I would cry or scream instead of words coming out. I told myself repeatedly that everything was going to be fine. Except there was always that other part of me that felt the emptiness rising. I wished things really could get better and stay that way. My life was a quadratic line, an equation with too many variables.

Another hot August afternoon, one of those kinds of days that melded into every other, me and Jess were sitting at the coffee shop. She always paid for my coffee because she got a discount for working there. Although she called just as much as my uncle, I hadn't seen her in a couple of weeks. I used extra shifts at work as an excuse to be alone. I wasn't ready for her kindness.

Jess was pale with blonde hair, dim freckles across her nose, and new clothes, of course. She wasn't artsy like me, but was fascinated with my ability to create something from nothing. She wasn't a big drinker, though we did sometimes smoke joints together. I was a regular at her household and often stayed the night. I could walk into her house without knocking and open the fridge, though I never took advantage of her generosity. She also gave me the space to be alone without guilt.

"How was your date?" she asked, with her blue eyes sparkling. She knew how I felt about people asking me questions, but with her it felt safe, even if she would never fully know me.

"I don't think it will work out," I said, leaving out the details. I didn't want to upset her.

As I put down my coffee, the coffee shop door opened, and the sun hit off my face briefly. The sub shop guy walked in. He casually strolled over to the counter, his long hair flowing over his arms. He tapped the side of his leg with his finger while he waited in line.

"That man is so amazing," I said to Jessica. She eyed me, as I didn't usually gossip with her like this.

"Oh, that's just Dan," she replied. "He went to school with my older brother. He's like, twenty-seven or something. Apparently, he wants to be a writer and works at the sub place. My aunt works at the bar and he is like legit there all the time after work. He was nice when I was a kid, I don't think he remembers me, though."

"Interesting."

I glanced back at him. He had taken a seat with his coffee. He took out a novel, flicked his hair out of his face. That one simple action made my heart flutter. I turned back to Jessica's smiling face, so I could hear about the rest of her week.

As time went on, there was something about Dan that I could not get off my mind. I needed to see him, like a craving for something I had never tasted, a missing nutrient. I would go to the sub shop, and he would be casually standing there in a green visor, hair in a ponytail. Our eyes would meet, I'd ask for some more cucumber, southwest sauce.

I would sit in a corner booth and sketch the way his nose pointed at the end, the curve of his cheekbone. I'd watch him stare at me and I'd tilt my head to draw his eyes to my neck and pretend not to notice.

I'd leave my house when the world turned to darkness. I would go out of my way to see him, and most of the time it worked. He would sit at the bar more nights than not. I'd watch him through the open back door while I chain smoked cigarettes and sipped my dad's homemade wine from a reusable mug. His hair flew when he drunkenly head banged to the music. I laughed to myself. He was perfect.

Summer had to end sometime, however. I found out when school was starting from the newspaper. Normally one's parents would inform them of the date, but I only saw my father when he needed me to pick up something from the store or when he wanted me to help him move boxes into the basement. When I was back on an early schedule, I barely saw him at all.

So, the fall I was turning sixteen, I started grade eleven at Sacred Heart High School. I was bored in class. I kept mostly to myself, except for the smoking area in the woods behind the school where I met up with the other outcasts and stoners.

I was too smart to be trapped between prom planning, fake tanning and what car people's parents were going to buy for them for graduation. I knew too much. Did anyone else go home to an empty house and rifle through the ashtrays to find leftover marijuana?

I found myself excelling through my schoolwork, but during class I often drank vodka from my reusable mug or from a water bottle. I usually ran home during lunch to smoke a joint, and sometimes didn't go back to class at all. Most of the time, no one seemed to notice or care. I wondered if I really had become invisible.

I started hanging out with Josh, a tenth grader who liked science. He lived in circumstances as shitty as mine. He, too, drowned most of his dreams and ambitions in alcohol and pot. We could really relate. Josh's father has been out of the picture since he was small. His mother had passed away a year ago, but he never talked about why. He'd had a baby with a fifteen-year-old the year before, so social services paid for him to rent his own apartment. He had the baby in his custody every second weekend.

Josh was tall and lanky, one of those people who was always sweaty. He had red hair, and freckles that made him look six years old. His eyes were always rimmed with red. You could see the blood red veins around his irises. No doubt an effect of the drugs he consumed around the clock. I always had a tendency to look into people's eyes, notice their eye colour. It was my way of shaking hands. Despite his troubles, he was a good person, and we spent most of our time together. After a couple of weeks of school, we considered each other best friends.

We shot vodka one night under the September stars. The weather was still holding on to the heat of August, like it never wanted to give in to the emptiness of fall.

"Dan's stupid," I slurred, the only words to my vocabulary.

"I know, I know, you've said that like a hundred times already." His voice was like a purr, the silly high-pitched laugh of a stoner, eyes glazed over from always being high.

I stood up, stumbled, peered down at the raging ocean. We were on top of the hill, so I sat back on the grass before I caused any permanent damage.

"Have some more," Josh gestured at the quarter-full bottle. I took it and chugged it back, stomach burning and eyes watering from no mix.

"I'm pretty drunk."

I passed the flask back, lit a cigarette and took an exaggerated drag. The tip glowed orange and then faded to black. I flicked it off, watched it blow away in the light wind. My body parts were numb, everything made sense, nothing mattered. I was free. I didn't know what to do with freedom. Freedom fell apart in my hands like wet tissue, when I should have been using it to soak up the poisons.

Josh handed me the last chug of the flask. I tilted my head back, the vodka slid down my throat like water, pumped into my veins, made me forget who I was.

I catapulted the empty bottle over the hill, heard the hollow plastic hit the beach rocks. A second later, Josh leaned over and his lips touched mine. In my intoxicated reality, I pretended it was Dan. I wasn't attracted to Josh, yet I found myself kissing him back, tasting the old marijuana and cigarette on his breath. Cheap cologne wafted from his shirt.

We finished our next flask of vodka and Josh passed out in a pile of trees. I turned him to the side, so he wouldn't choke on his vomit, and I stood up at the edge of the hill and yelled as loud as I could.

"I hate you! I fucking hate you!"
The stars just laughed and laughed. They didn't care anymore.

4

We got up to get some food and coffee, to try and sober up before we had to go home. No one would be waiting up for me, I could have moved to another country and it would probably take a few weeks before anyone even questioned where I was.

We went into the sub joint, and there was Dan, like a dream. It was almost midnight and we were the only people there.

"Hey," I yelled at Dan in a drunken staccato, stumbling. This was not my usual quiet demeanour. "I need some water." I leaned on the counter, my face looming too close to his, for strangers.

"Are you alright?" he asked, amused, the corners of his mouth slightly upturned in a smile.

"She's just really drunk," Josh replied, putting his arm around me. "Lily, seriously, go sit down now. I will get your water. You are pissing me off."

Dan handed me a paper cup filled with water from the tap. I shrugged Josh's arm off me and chugged back the water. It was gone in seconds.

"I want more," I mumbled.

I drank that, too, and went to the bathroom, leaving Josh sitting at the table. I was surprised he didn't follow me right into the women's room. When I figured out how to use the button and zipper on my pants, I looked into the mirror, my face distorted, eyes like fire. The image scared me, my cheeks plastered with red, my eyes crimson from all the pot.

I went back out, leaned on the counter, pointed a finger at him.

"You know," I said to Dan. "I'm not really stupid."

"I'm sure you're not," he said, amused once again by the drunken girl.

His eyes twinkled, that ocean blue with green flecks, like a tree growing out of water. My stomach was a hurricane just looking at him. I stepped backwards, nearly falling over. Josh dutifully stood up and caught me just in time, while sighing and rolling his eyes. I zigzagged back to the counter.

"Do you want my number?" I leaned over.

"Maybe we should wait until you are sobered up a little." The calming tone, the soft face. I thought of him in the black leather jacket he wore on chilly evenings.

I wrote my number messily onto the back of a receipt. I put my name underneath in my artist's scrawl, bravely left it on the counter, regardless.

"Can I have a bag?"

He handed me a paper bag, sub logo on the front. I put the flask in my pocket into the bag, so I could drink it on the walk home.

I took a lingering sip, and turned back to Dan, feeling Josh's jealousy from across the room.

"I have to go, can I get some coffee?"

He poured me a cup of black, half cold coffee. He never charged me.

Outside the door was a guy I knew from school. He was a senior and his name was Corey. He had his ears stretched with black spacers and his eyebrow was pierced. These guys from school somehow all hung out at the bar next to the sub shop. Corey had bought me the flask I had been holding. I hadn't yet discovered that the liquor store and the bar rarely ID'd anyone that could see over the counter. I took a sip of the coffee, then threw it over the guard rail. Corey was half done with a cigarette.

"Can I have some?" I asked, my head spinning.

He laughed.

"You are loaded, my dear."

"I love that guy in there," I replied.

Josh rolled his red eyes, giving me a little punch on the shoulder. Corey gave me a strange glare.

"He's twenty-seven. You are not even sixteen."

"That doesn't matter." I took the rest of the cigarette from him, and smoked it down in a way John Player himself would be proud of.

Nothing mattered. I just wanted Dan more than ever.

Once I made it home, I closed my eyes on my sheetless bed. The power had been cut off again, so I couldn't say how long I had gone without sheets. I had been washing the same pair of pants in the cold bathtub once a week. My father was in the basement with a few middle-aged men I had seen at the bar. The house was filled with the unmistakable smell of marijuana, the smoke floated next to my ceiling. I opened the window and lit my own cigarette, my head buzzing with alcohol.

I didn't want Josh, he loved me, but he didn't know what loving someone like me would entail. Loving me was a Rubik's cube, too hard to figure out, and not worth the time. He was too hung up on where he would get his next hit. He was too mellow. He was the one everyone called to hang out. I was just the tag along, the fifth wheel.

At my house, I was lucky if I got to eat. If it wasn't for working at the ice cream store and trying to go to school, we wouldn't have had anything. Nobody remembered groceries, and it didn't take a lot of intellect to figure out that men that stayed up all night and didn't eat, likely weren't doing something legal, whatever it was. Cars parked outside the house at three AM, AC/DC blasting from the basement. If my father did have any money coming in, I had no idea what he did with it.

I didn't know that we got money from the government every month to live in this squalor. We were the joke family, the people you stayed away from. The people you didn't let your kids hang out with because it would taint them. Little did they know that their perfect children were my daily tormentors.

I dreamt of him again that night, after I finally stopped thinking and passed out. His face, the hair that I fantasized about running through my hands. In my dream, he was always two steps ahead of me, but I could never get to him, no matter how fast I ran. I saw his hair disappear behind the bar, I drowned in a tidal wave of alcohol. I couldn't breathe. I reached my hand up for him to save me but he just stared down at me, laughing.

The week that followed, Josh trailed me more and more. We went to the city together to buy CDs and sushi, cigarettes. He shadowed me to the coffee shop while I drank lattes and drew. I drew the way Dan's silhouette glowed through the window of the sub place when we walked by at night, smoking and kicking around an old hacky sack.

He never called me.

Late at night, I would sit on my porch under the stars. I'd look out at the ocean. In the distance, there was an island, like an arch on the horizon. The sounds of the guitar I strummed flew out into the humid night, my voice sang along in a comfortable alto.

Your electric fire
Heats the places that are dead
The empty piece inside of me

I played while watching the stars burn, I swore I could see him walking down the road. Maybe it was only just a hallucination. If only he could have heard me, I was singing to him.

When I felt bad memories contaminating me, I thought about Dan, the way he could look so cool just placing lettuce on a piece of bread. I took Josh aside at school one day and told him I needed some space. Though he was visibly upset, it was too hard for me to think I was leading him on.

My sixteenth birthday was a few weeks away. Jess and I went to the sub place one night, and of course Dan was there, staring into space with that ridiculous visor on his head. I looked down.

"Six-inch veggie sub, toasted."

He was talking to his co-worker while he made my sub.

"Everyone knows that when you work a night shift you don't get any sleep. It is stupid to schedule me to open the next day."

He put on the wrong toppings. I pointed it out to him.

"I'm sorry, guys," he apologized. "I'm just kind of out of it today."

"Your subs kind of suck today," I noted, as a brief moment of sadness flickered in his eyes.

"That's so mean!" Jessica whispered in my ear, being as kind as always.

"He knows I am only joking."

We sat down to eat and he kept glancing in our direction. I ignored him. Why did it matter anyway? He didn't like me. He could have called. We ate and left. I saw him staring at us as we walked out the door, his eyebrows slanted in confusion.

5

That weekend, Jessica invited me camping. It was nearing the end of September, but we still had weather warm enough to sleep outside. One of her friends, a senior named Preston, wanted to "get to know me more." One of the things I admired about Jess was that she knew how to have fun without worrying or over thinking. In those days I strived to be more like her.

Her friend Charlie drove us to the campsite in his old red Ford truck. It was miles into the woods, outside of town, down a long dirt road. We had to ditch the truck and carry our coolers of beer and our tents down another walking trail. There was a large clearing, where it seemed like half the school was already gathered.

I was too shy in groups, so I cracked a beer, drank it back and threw the empty bottle into the trees. Some of the guys were throwing a football and the girls stood around watching them, whispering to each other. I sat in a lawn chair in front of the early evening campfire, put my beer in the drink holder and sketched the burning twigs, how they blackened and flew away.

"What are you drawing?"

"Not much," I replied, closing my sketch book. Someone sat in the chair next to mine as I stared into the fire.

This was the new guy, Preston, trying to pry his way into my life. The fire burned my face, like his eyes into my profile.

"So, you draw a lot?"

"Yes sir."

The flames told me to be happy. Flecks of embers sailed through the air above our heads.

"Would you like some of my drink?" He offered his mug to me.

"What is it?" I took a prolonged sip, the familiar taste flowing into my blood.

"Guess."

"Gin and fruit juice?" Who did he think he was, asking me to guess the contents of his drink?

He smiled, I cringed.

"Cream soda and vodka."

I knew I could have made him kiss my shoe, just with the way my green and yellow eyes twinkled and how my small back curved slightly in my tight shirt.

"Can I have a couple of shots?" I asked, already knowing the answer.

"Well, I don't have much left."

I looked at him, blinked my eyelashes and smiled.

"But it's not a problem for you."

Men were stupid, this was so easy. I could do this for the rest of my life. I would pretend I would give them what they wanted, just to get what I wanted instead. Then I would lie, disappear, with no warning. I would break hearts and ruin lives. I would never think of tomorrow. I would be like all the men of the world.

We walked to his tent and he pulled the flask from his bag, already half empty. I unscrewed the cap, took three shots in one go. I handed it back and he looked at me, impressed. I shrugged as if it were nothing. I could drink a lot more than any other girl I knew, most guys even.

I fell onto the grass and opened another beer. This was the routine, every night filled with alcohol, killing reality.

Maybe I drank too much, but I ended up in the tent with him after it got dark. He had his arm slung across my chest, his lips were soft, mouth like silk. He smelled clean, and like some sort of expensive cologne, the smell of man. Drinking was too dangerous, you broke your rules, and you fantasized. The hand groping me wasn't just another guy, it was salvation, it was hope, and it was something that had finally come to rescue me.

He brushed my cheek gently with the back of his fingers before he spoke.

"I am so sick of everyone asking me what I am doing when I graduate, I don't even know what I am doing now. I haven't had such a perfect day in so long."

"I know what you mean." I peered into his piercing blue eyes. "It's just getting through every day now, working, going to school, trying to make some art."

"You know, I have been looking at you since school started, you seem so creative. I love art, but I am no good at making it. You are incredible."

"What kind of art do you like?" I asked, deflecting the compliment.

"Anything that takes me away from here. My parents divorced so long ago that I barely remember being a family. My dad's girlfriend is a total bitch and she can't wait for me to move out so she can have a craft room. I'll probably just join the army. Whatever it takes to get out of here."

I took a moment to process the moonlight glowing through the tent, the way his eyes looked into mine, waiting for a response.

"I want to do the same. I am not sure where I will go. I have an uncle across the country who said I could move there anytime. I'm sure I could get a job at a little café or something for now. My dad won't notice anyway."

He stroked my face again, and took a breath.

"I have to say again, this is the best night in a long time. I never want to leave. But we should get back to the others before they start teasing us."

He smiled, and kissed me gently on the lips. It tingled and woke something in me that I never knew about. I took a photograph in my memory, of how he brushed the hair away from my face before giving me his hand to help me up.

Everybody eventually gathered around the fire, sufficiently trashed, and we passed around joints and fat Cuban cigars. We were having one big conversation, laughing and joking. I sat on Preston's lap and he held my hand, stroked my thigh. I paid attention to the conversation, laughed at the appropriate moments, and stored this good time inside my head for when I knew I would inevitably need it. Happy memories were few and far between.

I felt Preston's eyes blaze into my face, felt his body tense up as he touched me. I drank more beer and conversed with some of the people around me, about this teacher and that book. I memorized everything about that moment. The fire, how dark it was in the forest, as if you could go into the trees and never return. The smell of him beneath me and the way he made me excited to be alive.

We went off into another part of the clearing and lay down in the grass to look at the night stars. They looked so much better from here than I ever saw them. It was like my sky had been opened up to reveal a whole new galaxy that I had failed to see in the past.

It was beautiful, the whole fucking night. I put my hate aside. Under the stars that night there was nothing inside of me that was a secret. I said how lonely I was, how much I hated my life. He said he had a hard time as well. As I looked up, I saw a million balls of fire and for the first time, a million opportunities.

A shooting star streaked across the sky and disappeared, leaving its momentary trail before dissipating to nothingness. I made my wish.

"Did you see that?" he whispered, eyes twinkling like the many stars, making me catch my breath.

"Yeah, what did you wish for?"

"Happiness. It never comes true, though."

I fell asleep in his tent, his arms around me and protecting me all night, comforting parts deep down inside of me that I never even knew were there. It was cold, but his legs intertwined mine. I could have frozen to death in that position and I would have died with a smile on my face.

He left early in the morning, leaving me with a kiss and the scent of him stuck in my hair and on my lips. He was in my body, my hands, my thoughts.

Charlie, Jess, and I all left around eight in the morning, after the sun was full in the sky. We had put away our tents and sleeping bags, and piled the beer bottles under some trees at the edge of the clearing. When I got home, I lay in my bed, tired, hung-over, and something else, too. Preston left me throbbing for more of whatever it was he had shown me.

I thought of how his arms pulled me from the water of myself that I had been drowning in, the feeling of security. He wanted me, too. Inside we are all small and lonely.

I got back up around noon, and walked to the coffee shop. I put my sketchbook on the table next to my coffee mug. It inspired me to be there. Sand coloured walls, those plastic plants flowing from the ledges, a steady stream of jazz music. Jessica waved and smiled at me from behind the counter, I smiled back, a conspiratorial glance. On the ride home that morning we had discussed the happenings of the previous night.

Dan was sitting in the corner table by himself, hair falling down into his face, novel in hand. Seeing him still excited me, made me fly. I drew him, how the hair hid his face like a mask, his shoulders hunched. He never did look up, engrossed in the pages of his book and, as I later learned, a decaf with two sugars.

My cell phone rang. I had bought it off some kid from school for twenty bucks. I bought minutes for it from the convenience store, but it rarely rang. It was Preston. His voice was like oil, swimming inside of me.

"What's up?"

"Not much, I am pretty hung-over," I admitted.

"Well, we are picking you up."

Dan eyed me from across the room.

"I am at the coffee shop where Jess works. I should be here for a while."

He excitedly told me he would see me soon. I didn't understand what would be exciting about seeing me.

We hung up, and I continued drawing Dan. The sun through the window hit him from behind, making it seem as if his hair was glowing. I knew I was not like the other girls Preston liked, with soft flowing hair and perfect new clothes, good grades, and on the way to a university scholarship with cheerleading or volleyball. Yet, here I was waiting for him.

I drank my latte, vanilla sugar sticking to my lips. Dan got up and left. I eyed where he had been sitting, then peered out the window to where he was walking up the road. He met a woman, and they left together. She was tall with long brown hair in a ponytail.

Preston and his friend Matthew showed up a few minutes later. He leaned over to envelope my small frame and kissed me on the cheek. I could see Jess smiling from where she was cleaning the counters. Good old Jess, so perfect and pretty, wanting me to be happy.

Preston must have doused himself in cologne, it was so strong I almost recoiled. It made me remember the shooting star last night, the sense of hope.

"How are you?" he asked.

"I am doing better now."

He smiled. I could just feel how much he wanted me again. We stood outside against the concrete walls, letting the sun hit our faces and sleeveless arms. Somewhere between last night and now, he had changed me. I wanted to stay in this place forever. At that moment, how his smile shone brighter than the sun. I would have done anything to make this feeling last. He once again brushed the hair from my face.

"Your eyes are so beautiful in this sunlight. It is hard to look away."

I smiled bashfully, looked down to my feet as he embraced me in a hug.

"I am so sorry we have to go. Can I please see you tomorrow? Me and Matt have rugby practice and my dad will lose his shit if I'm late."

"Of course, you have my number."

"I can't wait. I'll miss you." With that, he kissed me slowly again. Once he made it back to his car, he turned to smile and wave. I waved back and watched as his car pulled out of the lot, and until it disappeared on the sunny horizon. I had been so wrong. He could help me. It didn't have to end it here.

I headed home for my Sunday call with my uncle. As much as I hated being home in the daytime, I could never let him worry. The phone rang and I picked it up with our signature greeting.

"Ahoy, Skipper!"

"Aye, Kiddo! How are you? What's all the news of my favourite girl? Get any awards in school yet?"

"School just started like a month ago. But I might have a boyfriend, I think, or something."

"A boyfriend! Wow! Good for you, kiddo. If he doesn't treat you nice you tell him Uncie B is gonna whoop his ass! Oh, you're so grown up now, where is daddy?"

"He is just out, I am doing some homework. What are you doing?"

"Oh, I am just going to cook some supper here soon, and take Rex for a little walk. I miss you, kiddo!"

"I miss you, too. I'll be here Sunday, okay?"

"Oh, I wouldn't miss it for the world kiddo, be sure to check your mail now soon, okay?"

"Okay, captain. Signing out."

"Aye mate, talk to you then. I love you."

The next week with Preston flew by in a flurry of phone calls, kisses, tantalizing words, emails. I had found a best friend, someone I could count on, someone who asked how my day was. Someone was planning to take me out on my birthday. Preston picked me up and we drove around, sang to the radio. He bought us green tea, and we drank it parked in front of the beach. We studied together at the coffee shop after school, his foot kicking mine under the table.

After we studied, he would bring me to his house until it was bedtime. I was pleased to know that his house was modest, although it wasn't in disrepair. It seemed as if his dad ignored him, too. He looked into my eyes as we lay on his bed.

"I am so glad I found you. It's like there is a whole ocean of crap and you are like the mermaid. I have never met anyone like you." He made his signature move, brushing the hair out of my face, his other hand propping his head up with his elbow. "You are so beautiful. I bet we can get away from this town together."

"I would love that more than anything. We could always have each other. We don't need anyone else." I took his hand and held it to my chest, feeling the pulse of our heartbeats between us, the anticipation of our next moves.

"I love you," he whispered, before turning out the lights. He came back to lie on top of me for another kiss.

After being with Preston every day for three weeks, I hadn't heard from him in a couple of days. I called his house, I called his cell phone, I even called Matt, with no answer. I was so worried he had gotten hurt, or worse. During lunch, I finally found him sitting at a table in the cafeteria with the other jocks. As I approached, the table fell silent, and Matt stifled a laugh under his hand. Preston turned around to look up at me.

"Oh hey, Lily, what's up girl?" He ran his hand through his hair.

"I haven't heard from you. I was getting worried."

"Yeah, about that," he stood up. "Can we talk?" He gestured towards an empty corner of the cafeteria.

"So, what's going on?" I asked.

"I have been thinking, and I really just don't have time for a girlfriend right now, you know, with like all the games and stuff. I am sure you understand."

Preston had found a new girlfriend, somebody on the cheerleading team, somebody not as complicated. It all crashed down, I was in the crossfire of war, I was stuck on train tracks. I had no warning and I had let my guard down. No more phone calls. No more rides home. I was shocked into silence, nearly incapable of believing the truth.

Her name was Fahlon. She was blonde, with gorgeous blue eyes. She carried a purse and drove a BMW. She was popular and had a giant house on the same street as Colin. Beyond that I had no idea what kind of personality she had, other than tripping me up with her outstretched foot on my way to the cafeteria for the last three years. I know I didn't have the expensive clothes and fancy car, but I had hoped my personality would have been enough to keep him. Unfortunately, this was not the case. I became too numb to even react to anyone else but myself.

It was not my beauty that spoke to you
Not my green eyes, but blue

It was satisfying to watch the blood run down my arm when I sliced the milky skin of my forearm with a kitchen knife. I wanted it to show, I wanted to feel something, anything. When I took chugs of straight liquor, handfuls of painkillers, it assured me. Anything to feel something. These were my cards. All I got were handfuls of jokers, time and time again. There was something very wrong with me. I had forgotten that this was the game men played. I was just a pawn to throw out of the way so someone could claim checkmate.

The hours and days passed in a sea of alcohol and charcoal sketches. The drawings were nonsensical—an octopus with a tentacle around my neck, drowning in the ocean. The poems were cryptic and depressing.

Those eyes, I would have stared into them forever
They are not worth the razor blade scars
Decorating my arms
It's the way you tear my heart apart
How you say you're done and can so easily run

Although I was drowning, this time I didn't care, I didn't want to be pulled back up. I would have done anything to just drop dead. I hated everything, especially myself, Preston, Dan. There was no limit.

The fact that Preston didn't even want me made it so much more torturous. He was a dream I could never touch, a wisp of smoke. I wanted to have him back, even if it was just for one second.

My life was nothing.

I just drank until the memories seemed more like something I had watched on a movie as a child; like I was an amoeba splitting under the stress and dying, so that all feelings left my body altogether.

"I love you," I whispered.

6

October came from out of nowhere. The sky and trees were on fire, and all I could see was red. Inside I felt nothing. Summer wound down, the humid air turned nipping. I drank four coffees a day, and liquor by night. It was my routine, just to keep myself from losing my mind altogether.

That first weekend, the one before my birthday, I drank so much alcohol that the ground spun, my friends turned into blurs, and I couldn't quite make out where I was. My eyes were closed, voices circled around me, slurring English into a whole other language. Arms were around me, Josh picked me up off the dewy grass and made me walk, drink some water. I could barely function.

I ditched Josh, with his groping hands, and whiskey breath, and went into the nearby grocery store with Jess to use the washroom. The sun had just set and we were already tanked, drunk beyond comprehension. I was confused about the people around us, they seemed like one person, and nobody at the same time. I had to close my eyes to keep one foot in front of the other.

We went to the washroom and I got so confused, I tripped and fell. Later, the customers eyed us suspiciously as we danced through the produce section. They were making sure we weren't their children. Of course not, their children were at home on the couch with a cozy blanket wrapped around them, cup of tea in their hands, and working on their next mediocre essay. Josh followed close behind.

We stumbled towards two guys from school. They were working, placing vegetables from boxes into a bin so people could pick out their own rotting, small town tomatoes. We pleaded with them for dates and kisses. They warned us off and laughed at each other.

After being turned down by the produce guys, me and Jess took a minute to sit in the deli area.

"There is like, literally no point of dating, is there?" I asked her.

"Well, one day I want to get married!" she laughed. "You have to be my maid of honour and make paper swans and mix the drinks!!"

"I will totally do that. Just as long as I have a fucking date by then."

"Well, maybe when we are older you can take that sub shop dude!"

I laughed, but it was a kick in the stomach that I could not have him now. I suggested we return to our group before security threw us out again anyway.

I wandered off by myself, a feat, considering Josh had practically become my shadow. He was just as drunk as the rest of us, so perhaps he hadn't noticed that I was gone, enticed by his own world of unreality.

I tripped through the doors of Dan's work. I held the walls to keep myself up. I stumbled over to the counter where Dan was gazing at me, making my breath fall short.

"Can I have some water again, I'm drunk." I was so plastered I even had to say I was.

He handed me a bottle from the cooler, and I took it with lingering hands.

"I have no money."

"That's fine, just have it."

"Thanks, what's your name?" Up until that point we had never actually been introduced, he had my name and number but I wasn't supposed to know who he was.

"I'm Daniel."

"Did you lose my number or something?" I stated in a low voice. I leaned towards him seductively, drawing his eyes down my shirt to where I wanted them to land.

"I did actually."

"Oh yeah?" My voice was smooth and never missed a beat.

"I am an honest guy, I really did."

I knew all about honest guys.

"Well, do you want it again?" I stood up and held on to the counter to keep myself from falling.

"Let's wait until you sober up a little, okay?"

Josh walked in, right on cue.

"I was looking for you,"

Those sad, red eyes.

"Yeah, yeah," I answered angrily.

I felt the world turning black. Maybe I was dying, I sure hoped so. I felt Josh's tight arms around my stomach, the cold tiled floor. I wanted reality but it would no longer let me have it, I was too far gone. I was probably better off.

Eventually, I woke up. Josh had me propped into one of the booths and was holding out a glass of water. It must have only been about five minutes, but it felt like it could have been forever. I said thanks to Dan. I had sufficiently sobered up to walk on my own accord, and Josh and I left hand in hand.

We went back to the rest of our friends and we all lay on the grass. I wavered in and out, occasionally leaning over to get sick. Josh kept feeding me water and made sure I passed out on my side. I didn't know whether to thank him or curse him. They all yelled at me to wake up, prodded me, hit me in the face. I could only hear them from a distance, like they were a television show on in the background and I had fallen asleep. I only wanted to stay in this place, safe from the world and dreaming of death.

Why did I ever let anyone touch me? I looked into green, blue, and brown eyes and all I could see was danger. That night on the beach I had let Josh touch me too, I didn't want to, but I did. Now he wouldn't leave me alone. I wished it were simple, that I could just love him, but I didn't. I felt bad about it.

Inevitably, I did get up from the wet grass, it had become more sickening than comforting. I wandered to where everybody was smoking grass out of a homemade water bong—a discarded bottle of cola filled with water, with a small hole in the tinfoil that lined the cap.

"I'm going to get some food somewhere," I mumbled, head pounding and face numb.

"I'll come with," Josh added, immediately at my side.

"Fuck man, just go away!" I stormed off but he ran behind me, like a kid lost in a department store.

I let him come with me anyway. He was carrying a soda bottle full of rum and coke. If I had to put up with him trying to kiss me and telling me he loved me, at least I could get alcohol out of it.

We walked into the only real restaurant in town, open only on the weekends. It had a lame jungle theme with crocodiles and straw hats hanging from the walls. I ordered nachos and a Corona. I didn't get ID'd, I already reeked of alcohol.

I took sips from the beer and looked around, trying to ignore Josh's lusty glares. We hadn't been there for five minutes when Dan came through the doors.

His hair was down again and he wore an Alice Cooper t-shirt and a black sweater. He carried a red sports bag. I assumed his less than appealing work uniform was inside. I held my breath. He was amazing.

"Hey!" he exclaimed, turning around to our table and smiling at me.

"What's up?" I asked. "Did you just get off work?"

"Sure thing, I usually come here to grab a beer on the weekends. May I sit with you guys?"

"Yeah, please do!" Excited, I took a sip of the rum and coke.

He ordered a beer at the counter, Budweiser, came back and sat in the empty chair across from me, right next to Josh. He pushed the napkin of silverware out of his way and laid down his beer bottle, took off his sweater and hung it lazily on the back of his chair.

"I am going to run outside for a smoke, I didn't get a break for like five hours tonight. That's the downfall of working alone." He took a mouthful of beer. "I will be right back."

Dan got up and went out for his smoke, leaving his half-full beer to drip condensation on the clean table. His sweater still dangled off the chair. I would have brought it to my face to breathe him in, but I figured I had already crossed some line towards being creepy, and decided against it. Josh went off to the bathroom. I was so consumed in my thoughts of Dan I had almost forgotten Josh was still there.

The room spun. I drank my beer and became infatuated with the coloured lights strung near the ceiling and how they flowed into each other. Life was a puzzle, broken pieces that eventually came together. Sometimes a few got dropped on the way, and you were left with empty spots you had to fill with something else. I didn't really need anyone to put it back together for me, it seemed to happen all on its own if I was patient.

I thought Dan would always be far away, like the moon, distanced, never letting me really reach him. Now he was here, so close I could actually reach out and touch him in the flesh. Josh sat back down, eyes half closed, stoned, stupid.

I downed the bottoms of my beer. The nachos arrived. I stupidly talked to the waitress, so pretty with her blonde, shiny hair. I momentarily wished I only had the problems she must have. She was perfect. She laughed, her eyes like pools of water.

Dan walked back through the door and sat down in his chair, draping his arm across the back. He leaned casually and sipped his beer some more. His clothes smelled like smoke and subs. The waitress brought us a jug of ice water and three glasses, figured we could use it. I poured a glass but didn't manage to take a sip before I numbly tipped it over with my elbow.

"I am so sorry," I said, my eyes tearing up. I always expected people were going to get mad at me if I made mistakes.

"It's fine, Lily," Josh purred, laughing at my behaviour.

Dan mopped up the water with napkins from the middle of the table and poured me a new glass. He looked at me with something in his eyes, I couldn't quite figure out. I assumed it was because I was behaving so strangely.

"I'll be right back." I excused myself to the washroom.

My phone rang, it was Jess, I talked to her for a minute, told her where we were and that we were okay. That wonderful girl, so full of worry. I went back out, and thankfully, Josh had left. I flopped back down into my chair, put my elbows on the table and picked at the still warm nachos that were in front of us.

"Your friend said he had to run," Dan said to me.

"That's good, he drives me crazy."

"Aren't you guys together?"

"No, I am as single as they come."

I shared the rest of the nachos with Dan, and we ate in silence. I could tell he was like me—he sometimes preferred to think over talk, loved to figure things out. I could hardly believe that I was sitting here with him. He was eating my nachos. He was so close.

"I like you a lot, you seem really cool," I told him, words exaggeratedly drawn. He laughed, and then smiled.

We talked some more. I told him a bit about what the last few months had been like for me. In my drunkenness, a tear fell from my eye and landed in my collar. Dan wiped my cheek with his fingertips and put his hand on my back. I lifted my head to look into his eyes.

"Everything will be fine, I promise," his voice was as sweet as music.

"How do you know?" I asked him, after a moment's thought.

"Trust me," was his reply.

"We should go out sometime," I said.

He looked at me hard.

"Probably best to talk about this another time. Have some more water and get you sobered up. Here."

He handed me the water and took a pen out of his pocket and a new napkin from the holder.

"Definitely keep in touch, though." He wrote his phone number on the napkin. "If you ever need anything, anything at all, you call me, okay?"

He handed it to me, his writing big and wobbly like a child's.

"Thanks so much."

I put it into my pocket, zipped it up. It was like gold to me.

The waitress came back over and took our dirty dishes and beer bottles. She laid a bill on the table, with some mints. Everyone else had left the restaurant, and other employees were propping chairs up onto the tables.

"If you guys would like anything else you should order it now, our kitchen is closing soon."

"I think we're fine," I answered, still numb and not yet believing what was actually happening. I had dreamt of this moment for months.

I paid with a twenty, let the waitress keep the change. Dan tried to give me half, but I refused. We left.

We walked around. Aside from the couple of bars where people lingered in the doorways to smoke, and the occasional cab driving some drunk person home, the town was abandoned. The moonlight glowed on his face, hitting it in all the right places. It was as if he were created to exist in this very moment, as if life had been planned all along to end up right here. Every thirty seconds or so he would flick his hair out of his eyes with his hands, involuntary as blinking. I watched him, taking in every detail. As he walked me closer to home he started to speak.

"You seem like a smart kid, why are you always hanging with losers and drinking? I mean I have seen you around for a long time and I know it's none of my business, but I was just curious."

"Dan, I could never begin to answer that question, to be honest."

"You should try to write! It helps me a lot. Lily, I know life is not easy, but there is lots to live for. I promise you that things get better. Sometimes the hardest things in life shape us for who we are going to be. And the best people I know have the hardest lives."

"I write now, actually. And I read a lot of philosophy. I like painting too, and writing songs.

"I would love to hear something you wrote."

The stars may be listening
Exploding dreams into atmospheres while I sleep

We sat down next to the famous river. The moon's mirror image was on the flowing water, breaking over the rocks. I thought of how it used to be a glacier, and now it was a canyon reflecting the stars. How even the world can change after so long.

"I'm so happy!" he said, as he smiled and hugged me. Perhaps it was time I started to try and change.

7

I finally turned sixteen. It was a Wednesday. I woke up in the morning, wished myself a happy birthday, and ate ice cream for breakfast. Dan even called me to say he hoped I had a good day, and Uncie B took that day instead of a Sunday to do the same. I was so happy I didn't even mind cleaning up the house and going to school. I smoked a joint by myself before I went to class, as my present.

School cramped my soul. I didn't understand how so many people could be in one place together, but still feel so all alone. Who knows, maybe it was just me. Invisible. I wasted away the day in the corner of the classroom, stoned. I sketched the backs of people's heads, how their arms strewn across their desks made perfect ninety-degree angles with the edges. I drew Dan's sad eyes, Preston's preppy haircut. I put my whole life onto paper, looking back on the pictures. But my life was so enormous, with so many burns, it would never fit onto a hundred-page sketchbook.

After school I walked through pathways and trails, crunching the brown and red leaves under my feet. The air was crisp and the days were beautiful. I wanted to bottle them up so I could relive them at any time. As sad as I was, I could still appreciate the beauty in nature. I drew the falling leaves in my notebook.

Every few nights me and Dan went for coffee. He often worked night shifts alone and I could never get to bed before one a.m., so I would walk to the sub shop and wait until he got off work. After he locked up, we would walk around town. We talked endlessly about anything and everything. He was a writer, had a degree in English. He just hadn't ended up finding a job he could be happy with. We both shared an obsession with cats.

"How was your birthday," he asked with a smile.

"A day I guess, I appreciated your call." I tried to draw his eyes to my chest, but he wouldn't look in the direction I wanted him to. "I mean, I am always just wondering about the point of life. I am so alone, after a while it gets monotonous."

He pondered for a moment.

"As I said, it won't always be this way. Focus on your writing, you are talented. How is work going?"

"I got fired actually. My boss is literally insane. Like, more than me." He looked sad for a minute.

"Do you need anything? I have food and stuff. What happened?"

"Well, the season is almost over and they close soon anyway, so I guess firing me was better than giving me a lay-off, then I could get employment insurance. But essentially, I was accused of eating a slice of pizza when it wasn't my turn, even though I had an eight-hour shift."

"Pizza?" he replied, dumbfounded. "What do you mean? You brought lunch and took a break like not during your break or something?"

I explained the pizza and no break situation to him and he was flummoxed.

"You should go to the labor board! That is so illegal!"

"I really am just too tired. I cannot deal with that right now. I am sure they will come up with another reason anyway."

We stood outside in the dark under the stars to debate human nature. My body was illuminated by the streetlights behind the sub shop, my hands above my head clinging to the chain link fence. He was so perfect. I would have done anything to have him. I knew it was something that could never happen. I leaned in to kiss him, he put his hand out, gesturing to stop.

"Lily, I think you are great, really. I just don't want you to have the wrong idea here. You are sixteen, and I'm sorry but you are not an adult. I am. I care about you too much to do this to you."

After that, I stayed home, watched local cable TV shows, and I drank. I drank until I could no longer breathe, until my stomach burned and I had not a thing left inside to throw up. Not one thought left in my mind. It would always be this way, until something good finally came along. I thought of Dan's phone number on the napkin and the words he had given me. I thought of Preston's cologne, Colin's stupid warm body. None of these things were the rope I needed to pull myself up.

I realized Dan could never be with me, due to my age. As much as he was an amazing friend, he also inspired me to make decisions for a better life. I put my stainless-steel flask in the junk drawer and started going to school. I concentrated on my work, only another two years to go and then I'd get the fuck out. I became an omniscient observer, a listener. Perfectly detached.

I dragged all the art supplies I had collected over the years out of the back of my closet. I cleaned my room; left my negativity where the art had been. I bought new candles and incense, folk CDs from the city. I set up my easel in front of the window. I spent an afternoon in the backyard building a stool with abandoned wood from under the tool shed.

I had acrylics of every colour, lead pencils in every shade. I had so much paper and canvas. I immersed myself in my art. That month I would produce more paintings than ever. I painted everything. I painted the walls. I painted my furniture. I made a tattoo gun from an old hair dryer motor and painted my flesh. I tattooed art on myself wherever I could reach with a steady hand. A music note on my leg, a skull on my ankle, a rabbit on my left arm. I turned my pain into one beautifully scary thing after another. I made my own ladder to pull myself up from this depression, by painting ocean floors crashing into waves, and burnt umber tree trunks.

I wanted to leave this small town. It held nothing for me. I wanted to live in the real city, but I didn't even have a job. A prostitute or drug dealer would have fit in just fine with the family I had, but I wanted to smoke pot with poets in Amsterdam cafés, play guitar in the historic streets. I wanted to lie on my own couch in my own home and smoke black Russian cigarettes, and drink Long Island Iced Teas while looking out into the city. I would have a dozen candles lined up against the windowsill and every surface would hold a beautiful piece of art.

There was so much I wanted, I couldn't even bear to think about it. I wanted real culture, the sound of cars with cracked mufflers driving down the street two a.m., drunken businessmen stumbling home from the pub on a Friday night singing old Billy Joel songs.

The phone rang. It was shrill against my placid thoughts and interrupted the flow of my paintbrush.

"Hey man, where have you been?"

It was Jess. Of course, she called on a Friday night, they always spent every weekend getting trashed. I had been too busy with my art to meet up with them. However, tonight I figured, what the hell. I probably wouldn't even drink that much.

"So," I asked, "where do you want to meet?"

"We will come and get you."

"We?"

"Me, Josh, and Katelyn."

I rolled my eyes at Josh's name.

"Alrighty. I will see you guys soon."

They arrived at my house as dusk was setting in. The October air through the open window was cold and replenishing. We sat in my living room and smoked a joint while Pink Floyd blared from my stereo. Josh pulled a forty-ounce bottle of vodka from his backpack. He was smiling that ridiculous smile of his, eyes surrounded by crimson.

When we finally left my smoke-filled stoner house, we headed to the main district of town, and into a wooded area behind the fast-food restaurant. It was too close to suburbia, with its cut and paste houses, kid's bicycles left in the way too green front yards, new minivans in the oil slicked driveways. It always just made my life seem worse.

Although I had left my flask in my drawer, Josh passed me the bottle from his backpack. I hesitated for just a moment. I briefly forgot the insatiable thirst I had for liquor. I felt the familiar burn running down my throat, the sickening aftertaste, the head-spin, the moment of guilt and then—the relief. We passed around another joint, chugged the vodka straight from the bottle, coughing and sticking out our tongues in disgust. I was drunk within ten minutes.

We walked back out of the woods, stumbled down the street, the streetlights blurring in front of my drunken vision. Tanked, I decided I wanted to wander around alone. I looked behind me to make sure Josh wasn't following me. He was engrossed in conversation with Katelyn, his arm around her. At least he had gotten the hint and found someone else to trail around and bitch at.

I ditched my friends—their loudness was causing my head to throb like a bass drum. I dodged around parked cars in an alcoholic haze, and loudly stumbled into some people from school. The jocks, the cool punk guys with their straightened hair and new converse shoes. The guys who dressed up to tell the world they didn't care about their appearance, the damn vegan smokers. Everyone passed around drinks and joints car to car. They were a large group of too loud and stupid males.

I recognized most of them from the smoke pit outside the school, or from ignoring or drawing them in class. A few of them seemed to be too old to be in high school, most likely the ones who purchased the alcohol. I talked to a few of them who were leaning on a car and smoking cigarettes.

I stumbled into a guy wearing a pink trucker hat. His striped polo shirt was missing a button in the middle. His glasses reflected the street light. He was leaning up against a red Cavalier and passing a joint to a guy with long blonde hair.

"Sorry," I said, "I am just looking for my friends."

"Well, I guess you found some," he mused, holding out his palm for a high five. I obliged. "Want a puff?"

He held out the joint to me, I took my signature puff—five small drags, tap ash, hold in the smoke for five seconds and blow it out.

"Do you live around here?" he asked, moving closer to where I was now leaning on the car as well.

"Not far past the river. Do you go to my school?"

"I graduated a couple of years ago, I'm in carpentry school. My parents own the thrift store."

"Awesome, I go there a lot."

"You can come with me and I can give you a discount sometime."

"I would love that. But you might have to remind me of this conversation. I am super wasted right now."

"Wasted enough to give me a kiss?" he asked, half-jokingly.

He leaned in and touched his lips off mine, his glasses brushing up against my cheek. My breath fogged up the glass for a couple of seconds, so I closed my eyes. Those few seconds felt like hours. I didn't want it to end. I liked it. I liked wanting. I liked having. I thought he was sweet.

His blonde friend appeared out of nowhere, I recognized him from school.

"I saw that!" he exclaimed, giving the pink hat guy a playful punch in the arm. "I didn't know you liked welfare chicks."

"Jeremy, fuck off," said kiss guy.

I never gave them another second and decided to turn around and walk home. I just wanted to pass out in my bed and forget everything. I was done with all of this partying. Done for good.

8

In the next month, I dropped everyone. I wanted so much to do well; I wanted to be positive, to follow my dreams. I even entered a painting in an art show at school. I got straight A's on my schoolwork, I learned to play only the best songs on guitar. I found a new job with better hours and conditions—at a fast-food place that sold only fries and hot dogs. We were not nearly as busy as the ice cream store, and I made friends with my co-worker Ashley. We would have broomstick sword fights while we ate the leftover fries that hadn't sold that evening.

One night, after I got home from a long shift, I answered the phone.

"Hey," a man's voice said, "I don't know if you remember me or not, but we met at the plaza last night. I just want to say sorry my friend is such a jerk. Don't mind him."

"It's fine. I'm over it."

There was an awkward silence.

"Well," he continued, "I was hoping you still want to come with me to my parents' store. If you're free."

"Sure. When is good for you?"

"I am free now, I can pick you up?"

I cringed at thinking of him seeing my welfare house.

"How about we meet at the coffee shop? I have to get something from Jessica anyway."

"Can do, can do, can do," he replied. I later learned he had a habit of repeating words three times in a row.

"Bye."

I got off the phone and scrambled to find something clean to wear, realizing I was going to miss my uncle's phone call. One week missed wouldn't be so bad.

When I arrived at the coffee shop, he was sitting by himself and waved me over.

"Hey," he said, pushing up his glasses, his dark hair messy. "I didn't know what you wanted so I figured I would wait to order. And again, sorry about Jeremy, he can be a real asshole."

"Whatever. A tea will be fine."

After he paid for our drinks, we headed to his car. It was a smooth ride with heated seats. We arrived at the thrift store, and he opened my car door and the door to the store for me.

"After you."

"Hey, Adam!" one of the employees said as we entered. Adam nodded and smiled.

We made our way around the store, a place I was so familiar with, and picked out goofy outfits to try on and laugh about. At one point he found a full-sized Donald Duck costume, the kind they use for parades.

"Well, I would love to see you in that," I told him, pointing at the costume.

He headed to the dressing room and when he came out wearing the costume, we could barely contain our laughter. He removed the head, holding it between his arm and chest.

"I think I will have to buy this," he laughed. "Why don't you pick out some things while I change, if you want."

Hiding my gratitude, I chose a couple of band t-shirts, a pair of gloves, and a winter hat. It was going to get cold outside in the next month or so.

After we left, we drove around for a few hours, sipping on our tea and talking about people we knew. I made him drop me back at the coffee shop instead of my house—I was far from ready for that conversation.

That silly nerd face of his, his eyes so green that he made the July grass jealous, flecks of sunshine merging with a colour I could not even mix with acrylics. He was quirky, slightly preppy, but in a way that didn't make him seem arrogant. He was twenty years old and I was sixteen. He always had money in his pocket, and he invested in his high interest savings account and RRSP.

He had rich parents who were ridiculously religious. He hadn't been able to party and live as freely as I had. Of course, he didn't live in a drug house. His family often travelled back and forth to England, as they were from a small town just outside of London. Their business was quite successful and I thought it was ironic that his family were the ones behind one of my favourite summer pastimes. He wasn't broken, he was a puzzle that no one had taken apart. He was so easy to understand.

We did the stupidest and funniest things. I told him how I wanted to be a filmmaker and he bought me a brand-new video camera. Something I would never have been able to achieve on my minimum wage job as a fry slave, giving my burnt-out father half of my money for rent. I had never in my life laughed or had as much fun as I did when Adam and I were together. I hadn't really laughed since the days my mother was still around. Now she was gone, as were the memories of her. I buried those in a very deep place. Adam made me remember what it felt like to smile.

We pulled up to the fast-food joint, and I videotaped as he ordered a large fish and chips, which did not exist on the menu. I loved that I could capture these moments to relive again and again. He picked me up from school and brought me out for sushi. We went shopping, and to the movies, he took me out to coffee shops, invited me to parties. He picked me up one night, drove me to the liquor store, bought me a flask, and the best brand of premium cigarettes. My calendar was full. I played guitar for him. Major chords that declared the feelings I had for him, rang through the October nights.

The night is dark, with the stars I'm not feeling lonely
There are no words to say, I just feel your arms around me
These dreams of mine are getting heavy

With Adam, there was always weed. He wasn't like Josh, stoned, dumb as a rock on the ground, spreading himself across his couch to silently play Mario all day. Adam was an animated character, he got stoned to comprehend things he may not have understood without the help of THC. We were natural together. Adam felt perfect to me. As low as my life was before I met him, it shot up like a rocket the first sober time I felt his lips on mine. I didn't need the alcohol like before, I didn't want to be numbed, I yearned to feel. Everything was going to be okay.

He paid for everything, the gentleman that he was. We would get tea or coffee and drive to the lookout over the ocean, the place where teenagers went to make out. We would talk, listen to the CD's I brought to leave in his car.

I told him everything. I let him see my house, even the dilapidated inside. I described my dad's beard, how the grey peeping from it matched his bandana; how school was so cruel that my heart raced as soon as I got to the parking lot. He knew I could only afford to eat free fries, that a very sick man ruined my childhood. He knew I rolled cigarettes from butts when I didn't have any money. He knew my biggest supporters were an uncle across the country and a twenty-seven-year-old sandwich maker.

Adam taught me to drive. I drove his car through the main road and subdivisions, down to the beach, into the next town. At first, I went slowly, staccato. Then there was the speed, the adrenaline. I can't explain how I felt when it was just me, the slick road falling in front of me, the power I held within myself to do anything. Driving was complete placidity, total hypnosis and meditation.

I felt so trapped by this stupid town, and driving was the first time I could fathom how I could have freedom to leave. I'd leave in a different way than the street kids playing guitar for money, their dreadlocks decorated with beads. I had seen them hitchhike through town since I was a kid, dogs in tow. It was like a secret club I always yearned to be part of. There were often groups of them in the park in the summer, sipping on cans of cheap beer and playing bongos. I tried to get them to notice me, but I guess it was one of those things you just had to be a part of, or you were not one of them.

Autumn leaves, sushi, laughter, kisses on the forehead, Ani DiFranco CDs playing softly from Adam's car stereo as we drove through the streets. Adam whispered poetic words into my ear before letting me out of the car, never wanting to let go. Sure, there were still bad days. Getting shoved into lockers. Now I always fought back. I never lost. I left before I had the chance to be suspended or get into trouble.

I wasn't afraid of authority. I saw teachers and principals as what they really were—people stuck in a nine-to-five job. People who go home to their big screen TV's, their husbands and wives ignoring them, staying on their own side of the bed. Miles of silent Egyptian cotton sheets between them.

One day at school, a girl named Jennifer elbowed me as I was walking down the hall. It seemed out of character, as she was quiet with nerdy looking glasses and braces. She didn't even hang out with Fahlon and her brigade of bullies.

"Fuck you, slut," she whispered in my ear.

I snapped. I'd had enough, it was seven years of that word. Seven years of torture from people that didn't even know me. I grabbed her by the back of the hair as she was walking away and shoved her into a locker.

"Don't call me that ever again or I'll slit your throat, bitch."

I threw her onto the floor, her glasses slipped down her nose. She looked shocked and didn't move as I walked away with my head held high. It didn't take long in the game of High School Rumours for people to know not to fuck with me. I wasn't usually violent, but I had reached my limit, and people knew it.

I still had to work five days a week, serving arrogant customers from under my own ugly visor this time. Now it was my sad eyes peering out the windows. However, I could no longer feel the demon of pain lurking in the shadows, waiting to overtake me and pull me with its full force into the abyss of depression.

I was only sixteen, and had been through more than most. Finally, after so many gruelling and lonely years, everything was perfect. I stopped scrounging the ashtrays for roaches and spending money on under-weighed, overpriced, bottom shake weed from the other kids at school.

I replaced my sorrow with Marlboros, a steering wheel, and horsehair paintbrushes. The person inside of me and the person everyone saw seemed to flawlessly merge together into one being. I was finally who I wanted to be. I had a sense of self again. The days flowed like my paintbrush on a new canvas. I felt almost normal. I knew I was the spoon that didn't quite fit into the cutlery tray, and I was okay with not fitting there.

9

Adam took me to parties on the weekends. When we were both off work, we often stayed out into the early hours of the morning. There was no one waiting for me at home, no one to reprimand me on staying out too late, or how my breath reeked of alcohol and grass.

Even Adam, at twenty years old, answered his cell phone at midnight when his mother wondered when he would be home, or wanted to make sure he was okay. When he got too drunk to drive, she would pick him up, no matter where he was, no matter the time.

Adam always paid for everything. I got to try some pretty good food, and new kinds of alcohol I had never even thought of. I learned I liked Porn Stars, Singapore Slings, anything fruity made in a blender. The drinks came with little paper umbrellas and sweet orange slices on the side of the glass.

I became a drinker of dry red wine. My favourite was Zinfandel. I ate spicy tuna roll and I loved fruit, especially mangoes. I'd never had the luxury of saying what I loved or hated. I hadn't even known. I had to eat what I could afford, drink whatever someone gave me. Now, I was someone who deserved to love or hate things. I deserved to have dreams, I even started believing that one day I could sing in a musical, sell a painting, and make an award-winning film.

Adam rubbed my back when I drank too much and got sick, and bought me greasy fast food that we ate in his car. We'd throw the garbage in the bucket outside the window. I wasn't used to attention, someone always asking if I was too hot or cold, bringing me hot green tea on the cool mornings before school, picking me up and dropping me off with a kiss and wishes for a nice day.

I always made it easy for him when he asked me how my day was; he was so sweet I didn't want to trouble him. If I got in a fight, if I got called a name or saw my own name slandered on the bathroom walls, I left out the details. For Adam, I was always happy, no matter what.

It was Friday and I left the doors of school to see him sitting outside in his car waiting to pick me up. As I got in, I hoped the popular girls looked at me with envy.

"Hey babe, how was your day?"

"Good," I responded, fluttering inside at his smile. "I had a science test. Pretty sure I nailed it."

"Oh yes, yes, yes. You are brilliant."

He put his hand on the wheel and backed up. As his head was turned, I could see the veins pumping in his neck. He started driving and laid his left hand on my thigh, giving me goosebumps.

"My parents and brother are out of town for the weekend, so I invited a few people over. I am going to head up to the liquor store now, if you want to come by and help me get ready."

"Yeah, that would be awesome."

"I figured you would be good at like, picking out some snacks to have, or something."

At the fry shop I would often browse my manager's magazines, the ones for adults who had money to spend on renovations, who needed recipe ideas. I got excited at the thought of being an adult who could one day buy ingredients for a recipe, or a couch cushion that matched a painting on the wall. He exited the liquor store with his arms full.

"I've got you some Zinfandel, and some of the sour shots for the guys, and some of these fancy beers, and this chardonnay for Melissa." He laid everything on the back seat, one by one, as if it were show and tell.

"Thank you so much. I'm looking forward to it."

"Anything for you, babe. Now, off to the grocery store!"

Usually when I went to the grocery store, I looked for things that were cheap—marked down stuff about to expire, produce that had a couple of mold spots. It was the first time I really considered that some people just put things in their cart without thinking twice. We had chips, crackers, different types of cheeses and deli meats, and pre-made hors d'oeuvres that just had to be baked for ten minutes.

I watch the rain on these window panes
The me and you
The molecular structure of time
The velocity of change

We brought our bags into Adam's house, and as we started unloading them, I felt like this could be my future. Preparing for a party, unloading groceries, cutting up cheese to place neatly onto platters, putting chips into bowls.

"A glass of wine for you darling," he said, passing me the glass, "thank you so much for all your help. Hopefully the guys don't get too wild tonight. They can be jerks when they are drinking."

"I am used to them now," I took a sip of the delicious wine. A bottle would have cost me a day's work.

We sat down on the couch, facing the living room window. The darkness crept in, and the rain started to gently fall.

"Cheers."

He held out his glass and I obliged. He took my face in his hands and gently kissed me, looking into my eyes with a smile on his face.

"Well, we have an hour before the party starts," he winked, as he placed his hand on my leg. I closed my eyes, wishing I could stay here forever.

A few hours into the party, it was complete chaos—shot glasses were being passed to me, Adam occasionally giving me another glass of wine or a beer, everyone yelling, loud music. I'd had such a good day and felt briefly guilty that I was unintentionally tanked, but I tried my best to keep myself present and not overthink.

The voices of Adam's friends circled in and out, my drunken mind not comprehending the topics of their discussion. I watched his face from the corner of my eye, taking a full-on glance every few moments. He looked so amazing, holding a beer, talking, smiling. The dimples on the left side of his face deep enough to hold my fears forever. He saw me, with my red hair, old jeans, wine glass in hand. He smiled at me, giving me a quick wink, a wink that would melt a heart made of ice. The corners of my mouth upturned slightly, shyness keeping me from breaking into a massive grin. He gave me a deep look into my eyes, as if he could read my thoughts, his eyes like X-rays.

The house shook with the music, a beating bass from a subwoofer settled itself inside of me and vibrated my frontal lobes. People I would ignore at school now all sat around, mellow and drunk. Different groups all melded together, the alcohol letting everyone put their guard down.

I never had my own group, I just floated among the plankton in the fish bowl, making my own set of rules, inhabiting my own coral reef. For the first time, they were talking to me. I looked around at the smiling girls and their sparkling earrings and teased hair, the jocks with their hockey jackets, names scripted into the sleeves.

I stumbled outside and fell into the side of the house, bumping my knee. The alcohol made my body ignore the pain. I smoked cigarettes with people I supposedly hated, who hated me.

"Li-i-ly!" yelled Jordan, one of Adam's friends, exaggerating my name into more than two syllables. "What's up!"

"Jor-da-an!" I matched his exaggeration, as he gave me a high five and playfully put his arm around my shoulder.

"You better be ready for some fireworks, baby!!!"

"Yeah, and you better not hit anyone this time! Hey, I am Melissa." Someone reached their hand out for me to shake. She was gorgeous, with long dark hair. I knew who she was but she never had a reason to speak to me before.

"Girl, it was an accident! You do some crazier shit on that cheerleading squad for the games!"

"Seriously Jordan, don't fucking start."

"Jeremy!" Jordan called out to the blonde-haired guy I'd first met with Adam. He got into our little unintended circle, and took out a baggie of some sort of drug.

"I've got the good stuff, and brought my techno CDs so this night is going to be on wheels guys!" He popped a pill of E in his mouth and passed one to Jordan, but didn't offer one to me or Melissa.

"Seriously Jeremy, you're such a loser sometimes," Melissa said, rolling her eyes. "Seriously Lily, do NOT mind them at all. Later on, we will totally ditch the guys and go upstairs to eat. They all just end up in the garage anyway. I'll introduce you to Katie. She will think you are just the coolest."

Adam surprised me from behind by wrapping his arms around my upper body. I turned around to kiss him, the smell of beer on his breath, cigarettes on mine. I cherished everything about that moment—the stars, his face illuminated by the light of the moon, the eyes I could drown in.

The night was soft, I felt light as a cloud, as if I could be reshaped. I was malleable as kneaded dough. Adam would feed me. Oh, did I have big dreams for us. He could drive me to school and to work, we could get our own place, make our own world, our own family. He was not picky, I could hang my art on the walls with no protest. I'd learn how to cook great food and we would eat supper every night together, candles blazing in the middle of our table. We'd make love under the stars, our bedroom window open to the moon. We'd fall asleep in an innocent embrace.

"We got some fireworks!" Jeremy yelled through the open door of the house. Everyone streamed out to watch the show, a few couples staying inside to continue their kissing. He walked to the middle of the lawn, fireworks in hand, and threw down his cigarette like the period at the end of a sentence.

"Sweet!" Adam turned to his friend, and looked at me one last time.

I continued sipping on my fruity drink. I went from person to person, continuing conversations, sharing smokes and smiles. I observed the tree root veins in Adam's sleeveless forearms pulse in and out as he set up a firework in the grass. He lit the fuse, and it sparkled before shooting up into the sky in an array of colour, making a loud bang as it went off.

The sky lit up Adam's smile. This was my life, and tonight I could actually feel it going somewhere. I was that firework, dark and dusty, sitting on the shelf until Adam came along and lit me with his fire. Then, I exploded, making my way to the stars, suddenly full of a colour and wonder I never knew I possessed.

It became chilly after all the fireworks had been set off. I thoroughly enjoyed the scene that had unfolded in front of me. I had been scared of fireworks from a young age. Tonight, I didn't care. I stepped into the garage. A crowd of people had also made their way in there, and it was hot-boxed with marijuana smoke. I lit up another cigarette.

"Lil-Ayeeee!" Jeremy walked over to me, taking a drag of his own cigarette, his pupils the size of dinner plates. "If your gold-diggin' ass ever gets sick of Adam, let me know. I bet you'd be a good bit." He winked and grabbed me by the privates. He squeezed, and then walked away wordlessly. Jordan laughed.

The noise in the garage became deafening, the marijuana in the air sickened me. I needed more than anything to get out of there, I needed to run.

Outside, the temperature had significantly decreased. Rain fell down in small droplets every few seconds, hitting me on the head, falling into my eyes. I found a dirt trail behind Adam's house where some of the teenagers rode their dirt bikes. I stepped around the puddles, trying to stay close to the middle in case anyone jumped out of the trees. I was consumed in my own world. I found a rock and sat down, getting my pants wet in the process.

I never cried, but that night I did. I just sat there in the rain and cried. It was hard to understand what I did to deserve my life. I was a good person. I held doors open for patrons behind me, I fed stray cats, gave homeless people my spare change and a hug when I went into the city.

I picked up a rock and threw it into the puddle in front of me. Water splashed on my pants to form a dark, wet graffiti. I got back up. This was bullshit. Nobody probably even realized I was gone. Adam had most likely forgotten that I had even been there in the first place. I kept walking. I knew there was a bridge in the distance, just past a tunnel covered in spray paint.

I stood on the bridge in the dark, the moon lighting the water below. I watched the river break into the rocks. I looked beyond to the lights of the houses, thought of the people that occupied them. I envied them more than anything—warm, dry, happy. Some of them were in bed reading, a cool glass of water nest to a small lamp on their bedside table. Content children, clean from their baths, happily watching cartoons and eating cereal straight from the box.

They were so lucky. They would never be broken, fucked up. I was standing on the bridge, the rain poured now, soaking me from head to toe, my hair dripping. I was too drunk to even know what I was doing, to remember there was something I had to do tomorrow, something I accomplished yesterday. I wanted to be that kid, parents waiting on them with milk and cookies, kisses, trips to the playground. I wanted to be the teenager who couldn't stay out past ten o'clock. I wanted someone to care about my life, someone to pay for my education. I would always have to do it alone. I wanted to be anybody but me.

I kept looking down into that raging water; it was a long way to fall. The water was deep, flowing hard, on its own mission. Once you were in, there was no way out. Nobody would ever find your body, unless it happened to wash ashore. Just one rock to your head and that was it. It could be all over.

I took a last look at the stars—the stars I trusted, wished on, and then doubted and cursed. They had been there since the beginning, they must have seen so much, that I wondered how they continued to shine. There were so many lies, so much betrayal, and they still stayed bright forever.

It should have given me hope, but at that moment there was no such thing, there was only pain.

I moved to the edge, wiped drops of rain off the cold steel rail. I locked my foot into the bars, swung myself over the top. I stood facing the water, as if I were about to take off into flight, but still clinging to the metal. I let one finger slip, then another, and another, until I was only hanging on by one hand. I made it to one finger, my heart pounding so loud I could hear it above the raging water. My body was warm with adrenaline, my face hot with sweat. It was the kind of feeling that only comes when you know you are going to die. How I wished that would have been the only time I felt that, but that feeling and I, we were friends.

At first this seemed like it would be so easy to do, yet I was still hanging on by a thread. Now I was scared. I didn't know if I could make it back over.

I slowly and painstakingly climbed back over the rail, so I wouldn't slip. I was surprised to find myself crying. I wanted to go home, I wanted to be wrapped in someone's arms, hold on to a teddy bear. I fell back onto the bridge and rocked myself back and forth, sobbing, so grateful yet still so sorrowful.

After some contemplation I decided it was much closer to go back to Adam's. I figured I would say goodbye to him before I finally trod home. I had been gone for nearly two hours. My pants were sopping wet, my hair stuck to my face in strings. I was so cold, the world spinning on its axis and taking me with it for the ride.

I went through the door. The party had wound down to a group of late-night drunks, and couples trying to find a spare bedroom. Melissa came up to me as I removed my shoes in the porch.

"Where's Adam?" she asked worriedly.

"What?" My heart went to my throat.

"He went out looking for you like an hour ago. Where have you been?"

"I had to run to the store for smokes, do you know where he went?"

"Well, he said he would be back soon, so I guess it would be easier to just wait. You look freezing. I have some spare pants in my bag, if you want to wear them."

"Thanks," I replied. "I really appreciate it."

I dried off in the bathroom and put on her black jeans, a size too big. I stuffed my wet clothes into a plastic shopping bag, and laid it by the door so I wouldn't forget.

I sat down on the inside steps that led to upstairs, next to the basement door, waiting for him to arrive back home. I checked the messages on my cell phone, using the last of the minutes to dial into the voicemail. There was a message from him.

"I'm freaking out. You were here before a few minutes ago, and now you're not. Call me please. Where are you? I am so worried. I am going out to look for you, please can you call me?"

Life was a fucking game. I just needed to play, figure out the best moves and cheat codes, how to get through the levels without falling down into holes or being killed by predators.

Adam walked through the door then, breaking my thoughts and bringing me back to where I was—sitting on his stairwell in clothes that weren't mine. Rainwater dripped from his own clothing, his short and shaggy hair now spiky from the rain. I stared into the dark blue carpet, the cheap kind they put into hotels to camouflage any stains or dirt, red spots dotting it every few millimetres.

I barely knew this guy, I didn't know his reactions, his temper threshold. What happened when he was really angry? Would he get mad at me, break up with me? Yell at me, or hit me? Would he make this one time an excuse to cheat on me, justifying it in his mind with thoughts of the one shitty thing I ever did to him?

Adam didn't do any of those things. He surprised me by taking three strides to reach me and giving me a large hug. He kissed me on the head, looked into my eyes, and pushed the hair out of them. He rubbed my back.

"I was so worried about you! Where did you go?"

"I'm sorry," I mumbled. "Are you mad?"

"Mad? Why would I be mad? I'm just glad you're ok!"

He lifted my chin then, raised it level with his, and looked again deep into my eyes. He kissed me, the beer on his breath lingering in my nose.

I really didn't mean for it to happen, but a tear fell from my eye and rolled down my cheek for the third time that night. I couldn't help it. I thought of what would have happened if I had really died. I didn't want to, but I really cared about Adam. I was falling in love.

His eyes, how he took side glances at me while he was driving, taking one hand off the steering wheel to lay in the middle so I could put mine on top of his. How he looked at me while I was sketching, as if I were some sort of genius or the most beautiful thing on the planet. I loved the veins in his arms, the dimples in his cheeks, the way he made me laugh. Finally, I had someone who wouldn't throw me away, or let my hand go as I fell into a bottomless pit.

"I need something to drink," I said into his hair. My throat burned, but at least nothing was spinning anymore.

"Want to come upstairs?"

"Okay." I followed him up, grabbed his hand in mine.

He changed his clothes and dried off and we went back out into the kitchen. I felt like a child, being looked after like this. It was a good feeling. He poured me a glass of juice. I thanked him in a cute voice. I sat up on the counter and swung my legs. He sat at the adjacent table and watched me with admiring eyes. I felt beautiful, knowing that's what he thought. The party still pulsed downstairs, but we were off in our own little world, staring at each other with a drunken lust and a twinkle of love.

I jumped off the counter then, stumbled slightly and laughed. He stood up and held out his hand to help me up and I pulled him down with me, catching him off guard. We both laughed, it was even funnier because we were so tanked. I wrapped my arms around him, lay on his chest, breathed in his musky scent, right there on the kitchen floor.

I closed my eyes. I couldn't pretend anymore, I wouldn't. Who made up my rules, about trust, about love, friends? Well, I did. And I damn well could break them if I wanted to. I was done. I didn't need one more ounce of protection from the best thing that ever happened to me. That night, I let it all go.

We got back up after a few lazy moments of hanging out on the floor, and walked past a couple making out on the couch. We went upstairs into the empty spare bedroom, with its generic décor, bare bedside table, and striped comforter.

I flopped onto the bed, exhausted. I could feel myself falling into sleep, black creeping over my eyes. I was shivering, fully aware my body was cold, but I couldn't quite feel it. Adam lay next to me. He wrapped his arms and legs around me underneath the blankets to try and warm me up.

"Holy shit," he whispered, "you're freezing."

I made a small grunt to indicate that I agreed with him. I knew if I tried to talk the words wouldn't have come out right.

"I'm going to fall asleep," I managed to utter. "Please don't leave me."

"I'll never leave you."

I opened my eyes to see the look on his face. He looked so brave, the slight indentation of worry lines between his eyebrows, the moonlight coming through the window hitting all the right places on his face. He started talking again.

"You are one the coolest people I ever met. Just be yourself. I love your art, you are so smart, and you know everything about books and history. You are just, like, awesome. Like, even after all the stuff that's happened in your life you are still amazing and beautiful and such a good-hearted person. Please don't change."

I was on the edge of surfing the alpha waves of sleep, his voice sounding far away, his words like a foreign language. I held onto the words harder than anyone holding on to the ropes while being rescued from the ocean. I repeated them over and over in my head. I promised to never forget this moment, no matter what. The last thing I remembered was his hand on my back, the warmth of his body against mine.

After that night, I hung out with him every moment we could be together. He told me he loved me, and I said the words back. They sounded so foreign coming from my lips, the words got stuck like there were marbles in my mouth.

Adam made me realize I never smiled. Adam understood me. He cared about who I was and how I felt. He made sure I was comfortable, never hungry, and always happy and having fun. If I was in a bad mood, he just knew and would take me to the park, push me on the swing, make me laugh uncontrollably.

When we had the opportunity, I stayed at his place, only if his parents were not home. They still didn't approve of him being in a relationship. If we didn't have the luxury of sleeping next to each other, he called me at night, the sound of his voice a lullaby, putting me to sleep.

I felt myself changing from an awkward teenager with clumsy legs into a woman with a figure. My facial features were becoming taught and defined. I felt I was transforming so quickly from an ugly duckling into the swan I was supposed to be. It was as if there was an outer core of my body made from dust that was blowing away to reveal something entirely new that lived underneath.

I could sense people noticed these changes in me, I felt eyes boring into my backside as I walked down hallways. I hated it and loved it at the same time. I started wearing makeup. I picked up the cheapest stuff I could find from the drugstore. I started talking to the people I had seen at parties and I made friends during school. I was so grateful for Adam. He had come to me at the perfect time.

Emerging from one skin into a much stronger one
I smile, though times have been hard
But I am still alive, willing to face the dark

10

I looked up. A ceiling fan revolved, making me sick. I rolled over onto my side. I was lying on a cold tiled floor. It was freezing against my bare arms. The tiles had small crevices with not enough grout in between, perfect squares. There was just enough room between the bathtub and sink for me to fit. Someone knocked on the door. I ignored it.

I laughed. There was no real reason why I did, something inexplicably hilarious. Sitting upright, I leaned over into the toilet and threw up, blue and red—something I had been drinking.

I had no idea where Adam had taken off to, it was another stupid party at some bitch's house that I don't think I even knew. Right now, he was probably off drinking with his friends, smoking pot. I hated drugs, they ruined everything. I was the biggest kind of hypocrite. I hated it and needed it, just like love. I needed the alcohol. I was afraid to feel real, but also the alcohol is what brought up the memories and the pain. Ironically, this was the only time I could feel anything.

My arms were plastered with goose bumps and everything went black.

The first sound I heard as I woke up, still on the bathroom floor, was someone breaking in the door. Music floated in, heavy beating bass, something by Britney Spears. There was the sound of a steady stream of urine, I could tell it was a man. I got mad that he would whip his dick out with a woman in the room, that he locked the door behind him. He could do anything to the stupid drunk passed out on the floor.

He walked to the door and I felt him looking at me, his hand lingering on the doorknob. He came back towards me, and leaned over to my face. I couldn't even open my eyes. It was Adam. At least it wasn't a stranger. I took his hand. I could see the redness of the burning fluorescent light through my eyelids.

"Hey," he cooed.

"Hey," I answered back, my voice deep and smoky. He gently stroked my face with his warm hands. It made me get butterflies in my stomach.

I slowly opened my eyes and he was peering at me with that look of gentleness and caring. He smiled, ran his hand through my hair. He had the most amazing smile, lips shaped like hearts and dimples next to smile lines.

I wasn't supposed to feel this way, not about these asshole guys. Guys that said one thing and meant another, guys that lied to you so you wouldn't be mad, guys that followed you everywhere because they "loved" you. Fucking guys that decided they didn't want you, guys that asked for your number and never called. Guys that fucked you over. Guys that didn't understand that you were just afraid and lonely, that you didn't try to be mean. Weren't they all just the same?

Are you home yet
Or only home among stars?

"Are you alright?" he asked me. "You look kind of sick."

I snapped out of my thoughts, back to where I was, drunk and stoned on a bathroom floor. The lights were too bright and my stomach wrenched. I turned onto my side in a fetal position, holding onto my stomach, as if it would make a difference. I couldn't hold in the pain anymore. Adam rubbed my back, and the sound of his rough hands rubbing against my cotton blouse made me feel even sicker.

"You're tripping me out," I mumbled.

"What?"

"Your... hand." I took a heavy breath, I could feel it coming up again, shots of tequila and one cent candies covered in sour sugar.

"I am so sorry," he replied.

I helped myself up with my arms, propping myself up to the edge of the toilet. So many nights and days spent this way, leaning over into somebody's disgusting toilet, so out of it I'd forgotten my own name.

I violently threw up the contents in my stomach, my eyes watering from gagging. Adam was still there with me.

"Just leave me alone."

I fell back onto the floor, everything slowly dissipating like my soul of ice thrown into boiled water.

How it all started
The beginning of ripping chests
That sense that caused
This chemical imbalance

I awoke lying on a couch, still drunk but not feeling as sick as I had been. Someone had thrown an empty beer can at me. It hit me on the head. I heard laughter reverberating in the background. I slowly opened my eyes. The room came into focus and my head spun slightly. I was so groggy. The numbers of a clocked glowed across the room, it was two in the morning. I couldn't see anybody that I knew.

I dragged myself off of the couch and found my coat, as I was freezing cold. I drunkenly put on my boots, zipped them up to my knees. I opened the front door to have a cigarette.

On the outside step was a guy named Zane. I had never officially met him, but had seen him around school. He played guitar and drums for the school band. I had heard he was a little rough around the edges, but from my observations, he mostly kept to himself and his set group of friends. He sometimes hung out with Adam.

"Can I borrow a light?" I asked, fishing a smoke from the pack in my coat pocket. I had switched to menthols.

He dug a lighter out of his pocket, held his hand in front of my smoke to shield the wind, and lit it for me.

"I am glad you're awake now."

"Yeah, I think I drank too fast. I never had much to eat either. It just kind of hit me the wrong way."

"It happens."

We continued our smokes in silence.

"So, you are dating Adam, eh?"

"Yes sir. We have been hanging out for a few months now."

"That's awesome, he's a really good guy." He took another drag. "Bit old for you don't you think?"

"Yeah right," I laughed. "We are only four years apart. In ten years, I'll be twenty-six and he will be thirty. That's pretty standard, and besides, guys my age are pretty unintelligent and we don't have much in common."

"Oh yeah? So, you have pretty high standards?"

"Well," I replied. "I guess you could say that. I mean, I am not going to involve myself with someone I can't have a conversation with. There needs to be some depth to a relationship, it's not all partying and drinking for me, despite what you might think."

"Well, that makes sense. I just assumed you were a bit of a flake."

"Gee, thanks," I answered back. "The first rule of life is: don't make assumptions."

"So, what is the second rule?"

"I'm still trying to figure that one out."

He smiled, bemused.

"So, what makes you so special?" he asked me.

"Probably nothing. I just do my own thing, follow my own rules, listen to good music, read, play guitar, paint. I don't bother impressing people. Maybe the reason you assumed I was an unimpressive person not worth talking with."

"Well," he said, "you have proved me wrong. I find that about this town as well, people are so narrow minded, it is hard to find anyone interesting so you just find yourself dumbing yourself down to fit in. I am sure you know all about that."

"Fucking right. After high school I am on the first plane out of here."

"Good plan. I don't think I am sticking around much longer than that myself."

We finished our smokes in silence, threw them onto the ground.

"So, speaking of Adam, do you know where he went?" I asked.

"Yeah, he went off with a couple of the guys, Adam is the only one that can actually buy alcohol and cigarettes, and they went to get some more beer and stuff."

"I see," I said, not bothering to hide my disappointment.

"Well, I am pretty bored with the crowd here. I brought my guitar, it's in the back room if you wanted to chill until he gets back."

"That sounds good to me. Fuck the rest of them."

We went back through the door, took off our shoes and I followed him into the other room. He took his guitar out of the case, and I took a seat in an abandoned computer chair. I felt this was the kind of thing I should be doing—chilling and playing guitar. Not partying with assholes to shitty music.

"Would you like some wine?" he offered, taking a half empty bottle from his backpack.

"I would love some, red is my favourite."

He smiled, handing me the bottle, which I sipped from. I gave it back to him so he could do the same. He picked up the guitar and started to fool around with some power chords, not really making an entire song.

"So," he started, "Pavlov walks into a bar. The phone rings and he says, 'Oh shit! I forgot to feed the dog!'"

I laughed. He gestured toward the guitar.

"You mentioned you play?"

"Yeah, not too well."

I took the guitar, adjusted the tuning pegs slightly. I was very picky on sound. He seemed impressed as I played "Stairway to Heaven". I was lost in the music. It was my favourite song. It told so much of a story through the music alone. I tasted the red wine on my lips as I played, my eyes closed. I finished at the part where the song got more electric and fast paced, slightly shy, as I was a closet guitar player.

I opened my eyes and handed the guitar back. He looked impressed.

"Are you fucking serious?" he exclaimed.

"I fucking am." I replied in a sarcastic tone. "Well man, I just don't see why people have to go around showing off all the time. Like, Adam has barely even heard me play guitar. I do it for myself, I don't want attention or to join a band. It just makes me happy."

"Well man, that was fucking great. I can't even play that song. And that's how music should be, from the heart. People are way too ridiculous, I agree."

He placed the guitar back in the hard case, closing the clasps, his shoulder length hair falling into his face. He passed me the wine again and he opened a window for a cigarette. He lit one up and passed it to me, then lit one for himself. He was pretty good looking and seemed super cool.

I took sips of the wine. We continued talking about music, and taking drags of our smokes.

About an hour later I said, "Well, I should go find Adam, I'm sure he would be back by now and he gets worried. I should give you my number and we could jam again sometime?"

"Yeah, yeah, that would be great."

I scrawled my number onto a piece of his notebook paper, got up to shake his hand. He was still sitting on the chair but then he stood up to do the same. That's when I saw the look in his eyes. The look I associated with danger. The look that meant *men*. The look that said I had something they needed; that said I was born to please them.

He got between me and the door, and turned me around to face him, our lower bodies touching. I was too surprised and caught off guard to panic.

"You're not going anywhere yet."

I struggled but he had a firm hold on me. He was much stronger and bigger than me. He threw me back onto the bed. I was in a state of shock, I couldn't even open my mouth. He put his foot on my stomach so I couldn't move, while his free hands fumbled with his pants. He got them undone and flung his belt to the floor, where it landed with a thud. I felt so wrong, knowing we had been in here for this long alone, knowing this was his intention. It was all an act from the beginning.

He stood in front of me and grabbed my head by my hair, pulling me towards him. I had no way out, my head in his total control. I didn't think there was a way I could get out of here now, I may as well just comply and get it over with. This is what life would always be like.

Then, a voice in the back of my head told me to be strong. Not let anyone fuck with me. A feral violence erupted from me and I gained the control then, kicking him in the shins. He doubled over in pain. I shoved my knee repeatedly into his face, and when he was on the ground, I continued to kick him, not stopping to see if he was alright, his pants still down to his feet.

I ran out the door and slammed it behind me, trying to get out of there as fast as possible. I hurriedly shoved my boots on, not bothering to look behind me. I marched down the road at a fast pace, I had no idea where I was. A group of people stood outside smoking cigarettes and laughing. They called my name but I ignored them and continued my brisk walk.

The further I went, the faster I went. I ran and didn't look back. What had just happened hit me more and more. I could have left that very night, just started hitchhiking, finding food and shelter along the way. There was no thought that was more appealing. I could have left right then, the whole world was open to me. The rest would work itself out in time.

I heard footsteps running behind me. I wanted to keep running, but was bracing myself for what was about to happen, thinking it was Zane, or one of his friends he had lied to and said I was just a crazy bitch. Then I realized that the worst that could happen was that I would die and the thought of that itself was welcoming. I didn't care anymore so I just stopped dead in my tracks and waited for what was about to come. I would commend the person who would kill me.

They reached me, I both heard and felt them from behind as they grabbed my back.

"Where are you going?"

It was Adam. I turned around and embraced him. The words of what just occurred were on the tip of my tongue, but I didn't want to cause any drama so I just kept it to myself. I was reluctant to cause him any pain, I hated to see what he would possibly do to Zane if the word got out. I didn't want to love anybody, especially not Adam, but I could no longer help myself. He could protect me. He could help me. I had missed him. Tears spilled over from my eyes and landed on his coat, I lost myself in his warmth.

"What's this? What's wrong?" He pulled me back so he could look at me face on, and he wiped the tears from my cheeks.

"I thought you left," I replied. I lowered my head so my tears hit my own coat, and so he couldn't see how weak I was.

"You passed out, I thought it would be better if I let you lie down for a bit."

"Someone threw a beer can at me." I sniffled and laughed. "It hurt."

He chuckled and grabbed my hand and started walking again, still going in the opposite direction of the party.

"Yeah, someone hit me with one too, I was like, what the fuck. Bunch of losers."

We laughed again.

"I need to tell you something, but you have to promise you won't get mad and start a fight or anything, I really hate drama."

"Ok, I promise. Shoot."

While we walked, I explained to him what just occurred with Zane. I expected him to be angry or at least make a comment of disgust.

"That's just Zane, he is like that, don't mind him."

I was too tired and sorrowful to even say anything.

I fucking said, No
This disaster
Every piece is part of my soul

We went into the woods at the end of the road and sat down in a clearing. I lay back in the cold grass so I could see the stars. Those creepy night time clouds spread themselves over the moon like a wispy blanket.

He had his arm around me then, and I couldn't talk myself out of my feelings for him. My heart had a mind of its own, and ignoring it was just as hard as trying to forget who I was. I knew it wasn't right, but I wanted him to sweep me away. I was tired of fighting and this was as good as I was ever going to get.

"I need help." I was declaring it to both Adam and me. I always knew it in the back of mind but could never admit to weakness as I just had.

"Help with what, babe?" He lifted his head from my breast where he had been lying. I could feel the cold air seep through my clothes where he had been, his absence defined by the frigid air.

I lingered over his question, trying to find the right words, the wind rustling in the trees above us.

"I think I have a drinking problem."

The silence deafened me.

He embraced me. "I know."

"What am I going to do?" I whispered back.

"I'll help you. We don't have to go to these stupid parties to have fun. I'd much rather chill out and watch a movie with you or something. You are my number one."

"Okay," I answered, satisfied with his response.

"Just do what makes you happy," Adam whispered into my ear, "I will be here no matter what."

I looked into his emerald eyes, and my heart beat faster, my stomach churned. It was never too late. You only get one life, and I decided to fix mine.

After a while, we both became too cold and tired to remain outdoors in our drunken embrace. Even my hair was cold. He walked me home. He brought me to my doorstep, and left me with a long kiss on the lips.

"I love you." The porch light hit him and it reminded me of how he looked in the moonlight at his last party.

"I love you, too."

Later, I fell asleep wondering what life meant. What love meant. I didn't really want to love anybody, but maybe it was time I started.

11

I awoke the next day to the sun slicing through my blinds. My head hurt. I was so hung over. Normally, I would have consumed a glass of water through the night, but I couldn't find the energy to get one after I had gotten home. My mouth was so dry and my lips were chapped and stuck together. My whole body hurt.

I slowly remembered what had happened last night, like déjà vu of a dream. I cringed when I thought about Zane, and felt just as bad about showing Adam my weakness. I was being so stupid. I shouldn't have told him anything.

Instead of waiting around for him to get up and call me, I put on a coat and scarf and just left. I would be the strong one. If he wanted me, he would come find me. If he didn't, I wouldn't care.

Orange and brown leaves blew across my feet and throughout the street. The sound of gravel under my footsteps resounded against the nearly deserted Sunday afternoon road. It was cold, yet the sun shone. The air was refreshing to my splitting headache.

I thought it would be stars and roses
At this time, the door it closes
How can I return to a dream
When I have been forever awoken from sleep?

I went to the coffee shop and ordered a large tea, topped it with ground cinnamon from the self-serve station. I sat down with my sketchbook and peered out the window. I anticipated seeing Adam's Chevy turn into the parking lot, Adam with wet hair, fresh out of the shower, wearing dark sunglasses—the kind where I can't see his eyes.

I opened my sketchbook. I hadn't drawn anything for a couple of weeks now, too consumed in thoughts of Adam and new friendships. I was too busy letting my guard down, driving around, stopping into restaurants every couple of hours for expensive meals topped with cocktails. I drew myself passed out on a couch with a knife in my chest, beer can mid-air, Adam standing in the doorway.

I sat there for over four hours. I realized Adam wouldn't come. I knew that alcohol would soak up this morbid rain, the perpetual gloom. It was like I needed to feel nothing.

I walked back outside, lit a cigarette. I inhaled the heavy smoke like a breath of heaven. It made my knees weak to feel my heart beat faster and my lungs contract. I loved watching the orange glow dwindle further and further down, until it reached my fingers, the filter wrapped in orange paper.

I crushed the butt of my cigarette under my boot, and I started walking. I was going further away from home. I headed to the nearest entrance to the trail in the woods, the same place where I drank with Chris, the same trail that, five miles down, I nearly died on a bridge the night I left Adam's party.

I closed my eyes as I walked. When would I get out of this small, stupid place? I needed the city, culture, intellectual friends. I wanted freedom. I wanted to be a woman, musician, philosopher. Never staying anywhere long enough to get hurt. I would move from one place to the next, playing a show, maybe taking cash jobs in a pub, staying in hostels. I wouldn't stick around long enough to meet any men. I would be the one to leave, always breaking hearts. I would take all I needed with me. My guitar, notebook, and pen.

Eventually I made it home. The day had been filled with dreams, wishful thinking and imagining. I fumbled with the key and let myself in. I was alone, dad's early evening marijuana smoke floating in the air, enhanced by the sunset coming through the window. If Adam wanted to talk to me, there would be a message on the phone. Either that or an email on the old desktop computer he'd let me borrow.

He had purchased a new laptop for school, and was just going to give it away anyway. He had come over and set it up for me—I was clueless when it came to computers. He had even found a device that plugged into the front that enabled me to pick up the internet from one of the neighbours. I could spend hours reading the online Encyclopedia or looking at pictures of famous paintings.

When I finally took the phone off of the charger and turned it on, there were no messages. I couldn't tell if there had been any missed calls—I had cracked the small screen one night when I was drunk. When I checked the computer, however, he had left me an instant message, though he was now showing as offline.

"Hey, I called you and no one answered. I went out looking for you. Just give me a call when you get this and we can do something. I love you."

I was happy he wanted to see me, happy he wanted to do something other than going to a dumb party and get loaded. At least he was doing the right thing by me.

He had only sent the message a half an hour ago, so I gave him a call. There was no answer at his house so I sat back and waited. He had probably just gone out for a few minutes, he would call soon, or show up in my driveway. I waited until long after dark, jumping when the phone rang, but it was only the usual bill collectors. My heart raced every time I heard a car drive down my street.

When it became unbearable to keep waiting inside, I left again. I walked the streets, smoking lonely cigarettes. I wondered if he would drive by with an apology and a kiss, I could sit in his car and blast the heat in the passenger's seat that had become mine. I wandered up and down the sidewalks, shivering.

I went back home for the second time that day. I slept for a few minutes at a time, waking up to check my computer to see if there was a message, my phone next to me on the pillow with the ringer all the way up. I slept very little, hearing his voice and replaying his words of "I will never leave you," and "I love you" inside of my mind. I opened my eyes to check the time and my computer every five minutes.

It's a mind I can't escape
No amount of love can fix it
These thoughts of emptiness
are embedded into my existence

Finally, after hours of interrupted sleep, the message light flashed on my computer. It was 3:20 in the morning. His name alone caused me excitement. I prayed he would have an adequate excuse for breaking our plans.

For miles, these wires always lead back to you
Follow those lines, right back to where you came from

"I'm sorry buit im rewally drunk. I loked 4 u but I cudnt find u. I went to a party I <3 u hop u r not mad plz I rewally wanted 2 hang wit u."

His words were processed cheese, canned asparagus. I knew Adam would be stoned and drunk, he really was no better than me. He could just hide it and pretend life was a party all the time. He could play the part. He was my part-time lover. That's all it was.

"Fuck you," I should have typed. "It's not going to be fine this time. I spent the day alone, worrying and waiting for you. Don't call me again." That is not what I said.

"That's ok. I'm glad everything is good and you had a great time I hope. As long as you had fun. I miss you and love you too."

"Im reli sry I luv u wel hang 2morrow ill cal wen I get up. Im goiin 2 pass oiut I had lkie 10 beer and a flask. I luv u."

He went offline. Just like that. I should have never gotten myself into this. I knew better. I was better than this. I was in now and there was no way out. Not when I thought of the way he kissed me. I craved it, I needed it, he was a drug and I was well past addicted.

12

I got up bright and early that Monday morning. I decided I couldn't handle the day in school so I just showered and dressed. I was going to hang out with Adam supposedly anyway. My dad had gone on a road trip with his sketchy friends. They left in their matching jean jackets, their long grey hair tied back with bandanas. Not that he would have noticed if I stayed home, or scolded me for missing school. I just liked to pretend that he would have.

To dream of futures
That lead into the paths of beauty

I cooked an egg and toasted some bread for breakfast. I paced around the house, waiting for my phone to ring. I played my guitar, drew a few pictures. Finally, mid-afternoon, it rang.

"Hey," he sang in his masculine voice, sweet but strong.

"Hey," I replied. "Sounded like you had fun last night. You were pretty drunk." I cringed with jealousy.

He laughed. "I totally was. I barely even remember what happened. I fucked up my foot, I'm not even sure how. It's so swollen. I left my car downtown and my brother had to go get it. He was so pissed."

"Cool," I said back, not really caring.

"Well, I'm assuming you aren't going to school today. I would really like to hang out, if you still want to."

"I might be busy," I lied. "Nothing is really happening for a while, so I guess I could hang out for a bit."

The villain of genetics only goes so far
It's the never-ending voice that always tells me
That everyone is going to leave me

"Alright, I will be down soon, I suppose."

"Ok, see you then."

"Love you."

"Later." I hung up.

We drove to the beach. I quietly listened to him tell stories from the night before. I didn't want to talk.

"You're quiet today," he said, opening his paper coffee cup and taking a sip. Steam rose to the ceiling of the car.

"I have nothing to say."

He looked at me while I stared out the passenger window. I could feel his eyes boring into my head. He paused, taking a sip of coffee and then spoke. "I really am sorry about last night. I actually did want to hang out with you."

I gave him a hard look, shot him with my eyes.

"I actually don't care, okay, so just drop it."

He was looking back at me, with those gentle eyes

"Do you want to go for a walk?" I gestured towards the trail that ran alongside the beach. I gazed longingly at the blazing sun.

"We could do that," he turned the key off in the ignition.

We got out. I took my coat out of his backseat—I had thrown it there when I first got into the car. We walked towards the trees. He took my hand and smiled. The sun lit his face like a spotlight—those magnificent dimples. I smiled back.

We took a long stroll on the beach, hand-in-hand. There weren't any words, we just enjoyed the beautiful day, looking out at the rolling tides and little islands off the coast. I watched the birds fly overhead. They'd land on the rocks that protruded from the water. I wished that I could be that free. I sipped my coffee and stood at the edge of the water as the waves went out, then I ran backwards when they regenerated and came back towards the shore.

When we got back to the car, he offered that we head back to his house. His parents were still gone. The sun was starting to set, and as we drove away, I memorized the red and orange glow from the mirror. I thought about how only a few short weeks ago, the leaves had been the same colours. The leaves had fallen onto the ground and were wilting away to make room for snow. It would be dark in less than an hour.

Upstairs at Adam's house, I sat at his wooden piano stool. The keys of the old Steinway were yellowed with time. It was so perfect. I began to play, a heart wrenching tune in a minor scale. Adam walked in from the kitchen where he had been boiling water for tea.

"I didn't know you could play," he said, taking a sip from a mug that emanated steam, laying one on the table for me.

"I can't," I replied with a hint of irony. I stood up and crossed the room to sit on his couch. I picked up my mug. He walked over and sat down next to me.

"You clearly can," he insisted. I laughed.

"If you say so."

The room was quiet, we sipped our tea. Adam kept glancing over at me, as if he couldn't quite believe I was there. I could tell he was falling in love with me, although I had no idea why. I couldn't help but to hold back a smile.

"Do you want anything?" he asked.

"A beer would be nice," I answered. Of course I would drink a beer, it was Monday night.

"Sure thing, babe."

He walked out to the kitchen and I heard him open the fridge, the sound of bottles hitting off each other like wind chimes. He twisted off the cap and handed one to me, then opened one for himself. The bottle was cold, dripping with condensation. I inhaled the vapour that escaped through the top, slurped in the foam and took a chug.

I found a coaster before placing it on the table. Adam's house was just so clean. He had a mother and father that went around the house vacuuming and wiping off coffee tables, changing the sheets. It was a world I may have once known, but I didn't have the best skills in keeping things looking like a house and home magazine.

He talked about something—a story of things he had done with his friends. I picked the label off my beer as his voice went through me, setting into my stomach. Every time I heard that voice, I just imagined how it sounded when it declared its love for me. We kept drinking and talking.

I laughed at his jokes, slightly buzzed on the five beer I had downed. My eyes felt half closed; my laugh reverberated through that large living room, half a second behind. I stood up, keeping my composure as best as I could.

I went back over to the piano and played again—random keys that just felt right. They came together to sound somewhat beautiful. You didn't have to know how to play to make music, it came from the inside.

Adam came over and joined me, laying his large hands on my shoulders. I closed my eyes while his heat and electricity flowed through me, a pulse in my body. I made him sit on the bench and I switched places so I could stand behind him. I put my small, smooth hands over his eyes.

"Play," I instructed.

"But I can't!"

"Of course you can. You can do anything."

"No, I can't."

"Please play," I pleaded.

He laughed, "Fine."

"See," I added, "you don't have to know how to play, just feel it."

"Fine." He reluctantly put his fingers on keys, played a five second song in C major.

"I can't do it," he said then.

"You were doing it just fine!"

I took my hands off his eyes and he swung his body around so I was standing between his legs. I never wanted anybody so badly in my entire life. I wished to grow wings so I could take him and fly, his cynical friends never again to get between us.

"That was pretty much the worst thing I did in my life," he said.

"Well, I will be, eventually," I joked, half drunk.

He was subtly surprised by my comment but I could pick up on subtle things more than anyone.

I sat down on him, wrapping my legs around his back. I shifted and felt him beneath me. It excited me; I wanted to make him feel better than anything in his whole life. I knew he was a virgin, I sure could. I had learned much more than him, I didn't want to stop now.

We kissed with beer breath and a rhythmic tongue. I clawed at his back while shifting the weight in my legs to rub against him. His arms were around my lower back, massaging me, growing closer to the edge of my pants. He rubbed my back with every motion that brought him closer to my bottom. I continued to kiss him, breathed in the scent I began to associate with Adam. He was the first real man I desired to be with, the first one I wanted to really touch me.

I leaned back, throwing my head backwards, he kissed me on the neck, my biggest weak spot. I couldn't help but to let out a small moan, it had been so long. This excited him even more. He sucked on my neck and I involuntarily tightened my legs, moving my hips slightly back and forth. He grunted, it was subtle, but of course I noticed it. I had been waiting for it.

His mouth connected with mine again in a lingering kiss, I could feel the energy cross between us and knew just what he thought of me. He only was able to see the beautiful girl in front of him. I put my hands on his face and kissed him so passionately I hoped he would explode. I stood back up. He assumed we wouldn't go any further than kissing, until I seductively asked him if he wanted to go to the bedroom.

He nodded and set off for the bedroom. I chugged the last quarter of both beers. I stumbled slightly as I followed him into the same room where had put me to bed the night of his party. I jumped onto the bed to lie on my back, hauling him on top of me. This was the same room from the party when he told me he would never leave me, that he loved me for who I was. We kept kissing, more sloppily this time. He kissed and sucked on my neck, extracting more moans and whimpers. I sat up, took off my sweater, a tank top rimmed with lace underneath. He began to rub me over my shirt, then under, slipping his hands under my bra.

He stopped to look at me. I never wanted this moment to end. When it did, I would not forget. I had never been this happy.

He slowly peeled off my shirt, never breaking eye contact. He undid my bra, a little awkwardly, threw the clothes to the floor, and felt up my back to places he had never been. I closed my eyes. I was floating through dimensions, swimming through a warm green ocean, flying through van Gogh's *Starry Night*. I reached over to him and smoothly pulled his shirt over his muscled arms. His eyes were rolled back to the whites, not quite closed. I could feel his yearning seeping from his pores and into my soul.

Adam kissed me through intervals of his heavy breathing, kissing my neck, kissing down my bare chest and stomach, my torso. He undid the button of my pants, slid them off, and threw them on top of our entanglement of clothes on the floor. He rubbed my nude, smooth legs, my hard calves. The black music note tattoo on my lower leg gleamed in the moon light coming through the window. He felt up my legs from the muscled calves to my thighs, running his fingertips over my body.

"You better have a condom," I whispered into his neck.

"I sure do," he said back, taking one out of his wallet. The first one he ever used with a woman. He kicked off his pants and boxers, not bothering to check where they landed.

I leaned back so my head hit the pillow, and he came towards me. It seemed like everything was in slow motion. I loved this man, I wanted him inside of me, all to myself. I would be the one to take his virginity, he would never forget me.

We floated among the stars and the moon, my moans piercing the quiet, beautiful night. He leaned down to kiss me.

"I love you," he whispered.

Afterwards, we lay on top of the bed with the window open. We were both hot and sticky. I cuddled into his sweaty torso and breathed in his scent. Nothing else mattered. I lay on my side, my head on his bare chest, naked legs around his body. I hoped he noticed how my tan back curved. The golden pendant dangling between my breasts.

13

After that night our bond grew stronger, to the discontentment of his shit-head friends. The following Wednesday, I invited him to hang out with me, Jess, and Katelyn. I wanted their approval.

I had actually gone to school that day, and somehow managed to get through it without any drugs or alcohol. I had, in fact, kind of enjoyed the day. People from Adam's parties said hello to me in the hallways. No one called me names and moved out of my way as I walked to class. My daily morning headache dissipated into the air of lunchtime. I sat with Corey—the punk guy who bought me flasks—and his friends. Things seemed to be going extremely well.

Later that evening, I wavered in front of the mirror, smoothing down my plaid dress and finishing off my attempt at curling my shoulder length hair. Adam knocked on my front door, and led me by the hand to his car. He always opened the door for me. We drove to the grocery store, to pick up bags of chips and chocolate bars for later, and a pack of smokes for me. Only the best premium cigarettes now. He always paid for everything. I wouldn't have been at all surprised to find out his mom still gave him an allowance. I found myself saving a lot of money. I was still working thirty hours a week, and Adam spent his never-ending supply of money solely on keeping me happy.

"I feel like a tool," I said as we walked in, people eyeing me.

"You look great," he offered. "People are going to look at you because you are so hot." He poked me in the side to tickle me, and laughed.

We then drove to Katelyn's house, and parked outside her door. Adam blew on the horn and she came out, locking her front door behind her. She lived a life similar to mine. Her parents had divorced when she was twelve, but she lived with her mom. Her brother lived with her dad. Her mom lived at the bars, blowing all her hard-earned money on scratch tickets and beer.

The big difference between me and Katelyn was that she would always see the good in a situation. She wouldn't complain that her mother was an alcoholic, but would be content in knowing that she wasn't dead. Besides, I was motherless, and there are just some things that can only be understood by other people without mothers.

"Hey, man!" she said as she climbed into the back seat. She rolled the window down a couple of inches, lit up a cigarette, and blew her smoke through the small crack. I followed her lead and did the same, letting the plastic and health risk insert from my new pack fall out the window and blow away.

We drove to go pick up Jessica. I rifled through my CD case, which had become a permanent fixture of Adam's car. I put on a Cannibal Corpse CD, a sadistic dark metal band with a deep growler of a singer. I turned it up on blast, making sure the bass was on full so it could be felt beating to the core of my being. Once Jessica got in, the scent of a light flowery perfume wafted in the air. We drove around, mindlessly chatting back and forth, lighting cigarettes and joints, passing them around to each other.

They took out the snacks from the plastic grocery bags and we ate the shit food, so good when stoned. Adam caressed my hand from where it rested on top of the gear shift. His car was an automatic but he always laid his right hand on the gear shift so it appeared he was driving a standard. It was just one of those things that Adam did that I noticed and thought about.

Did he notice how I put my paintbrushes in water to soften them up before I painted, or how I laid my ashtray on the windowsill? Did anyone see how I cut up my apples in boats, arranging them on the plate in a spiral like my mother used to?

Eventually, we pulled into the parking lot of the beer store, and pooled our change for two dozen beers. Adam slyly slipped my money back into my hand, giving me a wink.

"So, what do you think?" I asked my friends while Adam was in the store.

"He's really cool, man!" Katelyn exclaimed. She always talked as if she were excited about whatever she was saying.

"Well, I knew him for a while, he is so nice," Jessica added in her formal voice. She sounded like a scholar, no matter how stoned or drunk she became.

I stared at myself in the side mirror of the car.

"I think so, too."

Adam trotted back out to the car, cans of beer in hand. He opened the backseat to lay them there. He didn't drink this particular evening, although he did blow up a couple of joints. That was the major difference between Adam and I. He didn't need it to be happy or have fun, it was just an accessory of socializing. For me, it was the most important thing in life.

The three of us girls all opened a beer each and chugged them down, eyes watering. We each claimed a cup holder. I found myself at ease with the evening, not over thinking, for once. We all laughed, took sips of beer, lit up smokes.

I wished it would always be like this. The three people I cared about most in this world, the man I loved, all of us just having a good time and laughing, not worrying about anything. I didn't want the night to end. Adam eyed my friends from the rear-view mirror and smiled. He was so kind, he cared so much about everybody.

We arrived in the next town, a suburban nightmare I had lived in until I was ten. We drove through my old neighbourhood. The small houses were too close together and all looked the same. It was not the fairy tale I remembered. I used to think this place was so magnificent and full of wonder. I used to think that way about the world. I could remember a time when I would sit for hours reading, curled up in a blanket, not a worry in my head. Or I could spend the whole day with my box of craft materials, making one pointless thing after another. I had dreams. Anything was possible. I wanted to be on TV. I could sing in Broadway musicals if I wanted. How wrong I was about everything.

I changed the song on the CD player, a slow song done in piano and crying guitar solos. I lit a cigarette, exhaled as I rolled down the window, and opened a new can of beer. We momentarily stopped in front of the house I grew up in. I had first shown Adam where it was a few weeks ago. A house where I had been a baby, so helpless, and then a child not afraid to dream. Our family ripped apart by drugs, going from having everything to nothing so quickly. How fast my parents disappeared into their own troubles, forgetting me entirely.

I looked at the tree in the yard. It was overbearing on the tiny lawn. There was a shed my dad had built out back. My mom had once painted it brown but it was now done in new red siding. We used to be a family—a real one, with game night, movie night. Dinner on the table at five, my parents taking turns on going to parent-teacher conferences, drives to school and sleepovers. Putting my home-made decorations on the tree at Christmas. Going to the city's large stores and buying me clothes for school. I was size 6x when I could pick out my own.

I was drunk by now, having already consumed eight of the beer. It was the first time I had been this loaded since that night at the party, where I had told Adam I was an alcoholic. We all laughed as we threw eggs at as many houses as we could while we sped by.

We drove for hours. I chained smoked cigarettes in between chugs of beer until I had none left. I closed my eyes and passed out in the front seat, the voices of my friends seeming like a figment of my imagination, like a dream. Was I even real? Maybe this whole fucked-up existence was just a dream

After I woke back up, I pulled down the mirror to fix my messy hair and running makeup. We drove Katelyn and Jess back to their houses, now each sufficiently loaded and high. They stumbled out of the car with a goodbye and a chuckle.

After having all these memories of the past, I felt like I needed to see Josh, even if it was just for some closure. It had been weeks since we talked, I hadn't even seen him around school, as his attendance was becoming sparser. I had pretty much cut him off, out of necessity. I got

Adam to pull up in his driveway and told him that I would be back out in a moment. I advised him to wait in the car and keep it warm.

The burning head rush that leaves no visible scars
Except for the ones embedded in my heart

His door was pink with a little triangular window at the top. I knocked three times. Sometimes Josh got lonely, too, living all by himself when the baby was with his mother. If not for his son, he would have probably just died from loneliness. He used to have me, but not anymore. I momentarily felt guilty, but didn't I deserve to be happy? Josh opened the door in his boxer shorts and, as I looked at his face and messy hair, I realized I didn't know the answer. What I did know was that he would be okay in the end. He would drown his sorrows in weed, I'd have my alcohol and paints. We would all be fine with a little intoxication. We would all make it.

"Hi," I said softly.

"Hey," he answered, confused and surprised to see me on his doorstep, as if I were some sort of drug induced illusion. I looked at myself through his eyes, what I had become. My hair had grown out. Adam took me to the salon so I could get a good cut and even blonde highlights. The makeup I wore now to impress Adam, my curvy hips and flat stomach, my cleavage in the tight dress I was wearing. I had grown nearly an inch. My eyes were hollow with alcohol, his hazed from whatever he had snorted that day.

"I just wanted to see how you were doing," I offered, gesturing for a hug. He reluctantly accepted. He was so used to giving to me, he didn't know what to do when I offered to give him back something.

"Thanks," was his monotonous reply.

He shut the door in my face without saying another word. I stood there shocked and bewildered, yet I knew I deserved it more than anything.

I put my head down and I walked slowly back to Adam's idling car. I never looked back. Josh clearly had not looked back, either. Nobody ever looked back.

Divided lines of ultramarine eyes
Irises red, imbedded in our past lives
Before your worries were scarce, before those stares
You have wasted away your innocence
Our distance became glares

I climbed back into the passenger's seat and Adam drove away wordlessly. There was nothing else left to say in that moment. We went to get a coffee. It was a little past midnight, and nobody else was out. He drove slowly, while I laid my head on the window, trying to keep the beer in my stomach. We drove down to the beach with our coffee, drove in a circle in the abandoned parking lot before parking.

He reached over and touched my hand, sending a shiver through my whole arm

Take this disease away from me
Back to where is festered
Half-mast in my sail
But I do not want to fail
There are still a million stars in your eyes
A million hearts that will love your mind

We got into the backseat while the radio played softly. I was still drunk. We started to kiss, the situation getting heavier as he peeled off our shirts. We quickly had sex in the backseat of his car. It was much different than that night at his house. It felt like he just wanted to get rid of me, or that I was an object for his pleasure. Or perhaps that was just what happens after the first time. I didn't know. Whatever it was, I left feeling empty.

14

That Saturday night we drove to the city. I wanted to check out an exhibit at the art gallery. It was only a half an hour drive. Adam would never be interested in something like that, however he pretended he was excited for me. Adam was good like that. He was adaptable, he never had any opinions, he agreed with what I said and went where I wanted.

When we got to the gallery, I hung my coat up and picked up the brochure for the exhibit. I studied each piece for quite some time, feeling every feeling and motive behind each brushstroke, every part of the artist's soul that was revealed in the colours. I thought of how one day people may look at my artwork in this way, that one day I may be discovered. One day, someone out there may understand me. It gave me hope to feel other tortured souls, to see paintings of angry and furious black strokes on canvas. I received so much inspiration from just one painting alone, while Adam strolled through the gallery like he was window shopping, barely stopping to decipher the pieces.

This particular exhibit was by an artist called Ed Pein, a Canadian artist known for constructed spaces, as I read on the brochure. The entire floor of this exhibit was like walking into my own mind. I could hardly breathe. I was so in awe. I felt the anger, the contempt, but also the fantasy. I had used similar concepts in my own pieces. The scribbles that came together to tell a story. His art was pure anger and beauty. It was like he was a soul friend of mine.

"So," Adam said after about an hour of my silent art appreciation, "I am going to go to the café and grab a coffee, are you almost ready?"

"I'm not sure," I added. "This is my favourite artist. His exhibit has never been here before, and probably won't again."

"Alright," Adam added impatiently. "Just meet me there when you're ready."

Being around art made me feel free. I felt understood. I was finally not the only person fighting invisible battles.

I took a seat at one of the benches, ignored the people quietly eyeing the artwork, and the security guard standing dutifully in one spot. I retrieved my notebook and a pen from my bag.

There are a thousand poems left to write
There's an entire world that needs your rhymes
There are a million nights that need the stars in your eyes

After some time, I remembered where I was and that Adam was probably quite impatient waiting for me. Those few moments when I could just write made the world disappear more than any drug I had ever taken. I got back up and went to café, located on the third floor of the gallery. Adam waved from the corner, an empty cup on the table in front of him.

"Good coffee?" I asked, gesturing to the mug.

"Great. I am so glad you are ready, though, I am bored out of my mind."

"Yeah, I wouldn't mind getting out of here now. It is too quiet," I laughed.

"Cool."

He got up and we took the elevator downstairs to the coat room, and went back out into the cold night. Adam leaned over to kiss me on the cheek. I talked excitedly about my favourite paintings, and asked his opinion about what he thought.

"They were nice," was his reply.

"Yes, that is obvious, but how did they make you feel?"

"Well, I don't know. I guess I felt the artist is good. And all that stuff, you know."

"But did you see the way he painted faces so distorted, didn't you wonder what he thought of the world?"

"I guess."

"Do you ever think about colour?" I challenged. "Say, look at that tree there. Most people would say it is just green, but if you really got up close you would see so many colours, not just green, but brown and black and red, and so many shades of green that it would take hours just to paint one leaf. You have to think of things abstractly—things aren't always what they appear to be. There is a deeper meaning in everything. Even the road in front of you is perfectly parallel with that building. You know what I am getting at?"

I wanted to reach Adam somehow, and make him see the world through my eyes.

"You are too smart for me," he said, laughing. "But I see what you're saying."

That night was the beginning of my dreaming. I realized that I needed to get myself out of the hole I had been living in, and do something with my life. I thought of people from war-torn countries, and strong women who could survive anything, and knew that one day things would be all right for me. I just wished it didn't take so long to fall into place.

As somber sadness takes its berth
I perch
On the axis of accomplishment

We drove the streets aimlessly, getting caught in the city traffic next to the hundred-year-old buildings. I watched the busy people walking the streets—couples hand-in-hand, street kids playing guitar. I knew this was where I belonged. I felt at home among the crowds and cafés.

I closed my eyes and inhaled everything about that moment. The scent of Adam's cologne and my cigarette smoke filling the car, my Italian opera CD playing from the car stereo. Everything about this place and moment was perfect.

Adam saw me eyeing him and smiled. Tonight, I could almost understand why he would want me.

Those nights of the thrilling desire to believe
That perhaps you could know me

"Are you hungry?" he asked, looking over at me.

"A little," I admitted. I wasn't eating too much these days. I felt self-conscious under his eyes, like I needed to constantly maintain the beauty he felt I possessed.

"What would you like?" he asked sweetly, glancing over at me and then back to the slick road.

I shifted in my seat.

"I don't have much money."

My dad had convinced me to lend him the remainder of my savings until he got paid. He had to take another trip out of town. It was either give in or have nowhere else to live, not that it would have been a bad thing to get out. I just didn't know how to say no to him, I thought I had no other options. The guilt he was able to layer on me about "all he did for me" always won over my rationality. At least with him gone, the house was quiet for a couple of weeks. So, it was worth every penny.

"Don't even worry about it!"

I stayed silent. It bothered me how he always had a lot more money than I did. I knew that that most people didn't live the way I did, paycheque to paycheque, buying their own groceries from the age of twelve. When I started making friends, I was jealous of how easy their lives were—everything paid for, pocket money on the side, a new car, a few hundred bucks for new clothes. I never had any of that. I didn't want Adam to figure me out. I knew that if he did, he wouldn't be back. I hadn't even let him inside of my house yet, too ashamed of what he might think of me.

"Have you ever tried Indian food?" he asked.

"Not yet," I replied. "I always wanted to, though. Is it expensive?"

"It's not too bad. There's a wicked place down the road that me and my family go to all the time. Do you want to try it?"

"Okay," I smiled.

Adam pulled into an empty parking space and we got out and headed down the wide sidewalk. The sky glowed with streetlights, and the air had a light mist that you could only see with the glow of the street lamps. I felt the mist falling softly on my eyelids. The breeze was crisp as I peered into shop windows—the tourist crafts, wedding gowns. It was an oddly quiet night, immersed in stars, the moon a bright crescent high in the sky. I was kind of like the moon myself. Sometimes I was bright and shining, full and wonderful. I would wane further and further towards disappearance, less bright and happy each day. I would be gone then, and right back to where I started all over again. A never-ending cycle.

The fancy set of steps had a brass handrail. The building's architecture was created to resemble an Indian temple. The lights inside were dim, a sitar sat on the ledge and high-pitched Indian music played in the background. While we waited for a table, they gave us each a book of matches with the restaurant logo on the cover. It was by far one of the fanciest places I had been.

I couldn't bear to let Adam buy me food here. Not that he couldn't afford it—a new car probably wouldn't make a dent in his account. I just didn't want him to waste it on me. I didn't deserve it. I didn't know what to do with all of this perfection. I just took it as it came, strutting to my table in my high heeled shoes, pretending to be somebody's loved daughter, this man's beautiful girlfriend.

The other customers watched me. My eyes were like emeralds. Little did they know it was the first day in weeks I had been sober, that I could never afford this fancy place with its pillar candles in fancy glass globes. My clothes were all free from the church clothing drive and if it weren't for this man I would barely have eaten today.

Our waitress seated us, and I nervously opened the menu. The cheapest thing was ten-dollar bread. Ten dollars would pretty much feed me for a week.

"Can I get you guys something to drink?" the waitress asked.

"I'll have a Corona," Adam answered, "and a Manhattan for my girlfriend."

She glanced at me, visually making sure I was of age while jotting down our orders. She walked away.

"How did you know that was my new favourite cocktail?" I smiled again.

"It's a secret," he laughed.

"Fine," I joked, crossing my arms and pouting.

"Well, I guess I can let you in on this one secret. You were talking about wanting to move to New York sometime because it's the biggest city and probably has the best alcohol. So, it was pretty obvious to me."

I eased back in my seat and couldn't help grinning about the fact he had remembered, and that he actually listened to me talk about one of my dreams for the future.

"I really hope it's not expensive," I said at last.

"It doesn't matter," he answered, "as long as you're happy."

We finished our meal. I took the last sip of my cocktail. I had eaten as much as I could without exploding. I didn't want anything to go to waste. My stomach had shrunk so much lately, it couldn't hold a full meal too well. I was slightly tipsy from the strong cocktail.

You are like my own drug
I don't want to know what it's like when I wake up
Even though it is known
That you aren't the missing piece

The waitress brought the bill, it came to over one hundred dollars. He laid seven twenty-dollar bills on the table, not waiting for change. I looked back at all the food I had left of my fifty-dollar chicken dinner. I didn't deserve this.

After we left the restaurant, we didn't go back to the car. Instead, we sat across from each other at a café. Daft Punk played from the speakers and we ordered coffees. I took a long sip of my coffee.

"Tonight was wicked," I told him.

"Yeah, it was rad," was his reply. He was absentmindedly chewing on an oatmeal cookie. A crumb fell from the side of his mouth and landed on the table. I watched it fall and then stared at the spot on the table where it had landed.

We left the café and drove to a store up the street so Adam could pick me up some beer. He parked in the lot of a fast-food restaurant, right across from a slew of three-story condos that had stores occupying the bottom floor.

"I'll be right back," he said. He got out and crossed the street to one of the stores.

I cranked up the music as loud as it would go and lit a cigarette. There were some teenagers standing on the corner smoking, and they glared at me. I ignored their stares, their disapproving attitude about the guitar riffs and scream vocals emanating from the car. They looked down at their snow-white shoes to make sure their spit hit the ground. They turned the brims of their trendy hats to the side.

Adam came out of the store and, after looking both ways, crossed the road, a dozen beer in hand. He almost tripped up when he reached the sidewalk, but managed to steady himself. I looked away, pretended not to notice.

"Long line," he said, as he got back in. I tapped my cigarette ash out of the half-opened window.

"Shitty," I replied, taking a long drag. I reached into the beer box, then cracked a beer, exhaled my smoke in neat O rings.

I chugged half of it in one sip as I eased back in my seat and crossed my legs. Adam was watching me. I could see him from the corner of my eye. I could feel his gaze on the side of my cheek.

"You're so beautiful," he said dreamily.

I turned to see him smiling.

"You're blind," I said laughing.

He looked down into his lap, defeated. He looked back up. After a moment he looked into my eyes with a new determination.

"Don't say that." He took my hand. I almost pulled it back, but reluctantly let him continue.

I turned away to throw my cigarette stub out of the window. I poured the rest of my beer down my throat. I tried to find something to focus my eyes on. I watched a man in the window above the store. He was bald and shirtless, sitting at a computer desk and immersed in the contents of the screen. He was oblivious to the fact that he had neglected to close his shades.

Blue light came from the room. He had one of those aquariums in the middle of the wall—I could see the colourful fish swimming around the fake plants. I opened another beer, lit another smoke, exhaled through the crack in the window.

"I love you," Adam said, making me turn back towards him.

"Do you?" I asked him. I felt anger rising inside of me. "Do you even know what love is?"

"What?" He warded off my cynicism with a sweet tone. Even that couldn't stop me now.

"Do you?" I vigorously asked, fire burning through my bright eyes.

He was silent.

"How do you know what love is?"

It's an unfortunate circumstance
How you always lose when taking chances
That you only think of past experiences
Somehow preferring the chase instead
Something inside of you is dead

"I don't know," he answered in a surprised voice, "you just like, know or whatever."

I shot him a look that would have obliterated Satan himself.

"Fuck love."

They were the crispest words I had ever spoken. My voice clear as the night sky, clear as the tears that fogged Adam's eyes, clearer than anything I had ever felt.

On my fourth beer, I turned to Adam and kissed him, my anger and brain cells now melted away. He kissed me back, following my lead. Adam had no personality. He knew what to say and when to say it, knew what to do, how and when. Who was he really? He had no favourite colour, ate where I wanted to, drove wherever I told him. I didn't have answers, yet I couldn't imagine waking up without him, couldn't picture not being able to flop myself on his couch and chug a beer. I was addicted to his nothingness, a vacuum sucked into space, magnetized into infinity.

I drank and drank and drank. He had bought me a dozen beer and I lapped up every last drop. I couldn't even breathe, I was so drunk. I wished I was sober, I wished I could escape the alcohol crawling through my veins, infesting my soul. I passed out in the seat, on the grey and stale upholstery.

My head hit off the window as he drove. I couldn't open my eyes, I couldn't move. I managed to lift my hand to the CD player and turn the volume all the way up. Adam's breathing was too loud, it gave me a headache, and I didn't want him to hear me moan in agony. As I sank into the world of intoxication, seconds seemed like minutes, minutes seemed like hours and hours seemed like days. I spent an eternity slowly dying in his car.

I awoke to him shaking me, lights blurring my eyes and burning into my skull. He yelled at me to wake up. We were parked somewhere. Slowly and painstakingly, I lifted my head to see an all-night fast-food restaurant. My head throbbed and everything spun like I was on some sort of amusement park ride. I moaned and closed my eyes again. The worst thing about drinking was waking up, coming back to the reality of your mind swimming through muck.

He went through the drive through and ignored me, thinking I was passed out.

"I'll have a bacon cheeseburger meal, cola for the drink," I heard him say into the speaker. The young woman responded through static.

A few more minutes passed—minutes still so long they felt like hours. I tried singing in my head to drown out the sounds of him eating in the quiet car. The ruffle of him unwrapping packages and reaching into the paper bag. Him loudly chewing on the greasy food. I saw him through my half-opened eyes, but he was a dream, a shadow. My eyes were so covered in the familiar boozy film, it was as if I were looking through foggy sunglasses. I realized we were parked in the dark, somewhere in front of a brick wall.

He had finished eating and opened the door to throw his garbage on the ground. I changed the position of my cramped legs, simultaneously hoping he didn't make me go anywhere in this state.

He slammed the door. I sat up and looked in the mirror to fix my running makeup. I numbly tried to work the tangles out of my hair. It was so perplexing how I could spend hours getting ready but by the end of the night I was always a wreck.

"How you doing?" he asked.

"What time is it?" I cleared my throat and reclined my seat, rubbed my throbbing head hard with my hands.

"Two in the morning. What time do you have to be home?"

"Never," I answered. It was what I always said.

"Well, I guess we can stay here forever," he joked.

"Well, I guess we will," I replied to his joke. He laughed. I was still too drunk to laugh, one of my eyes was half closed, and it wouldn't open no matter how hard I willed it to.

I grabbed his soft drink from the cup holder between the front seats and took a long gulp. I hadn't realized how thirsty I was until I took a drink. My head throbbed every time I moved my eyes. Why did I do this to myself? I just wanted one second away from it all.

"Can we hang out tomorrow?" I questioned in a raspy, tired voice. The soft drink sobered me up enough so that I could comprehend English. He took my small cold hands in his big ones.

"I would love that more than anything."

Adam drove me back home. I fell asleep under my thin blanket, still fully clothed, except for the socks I had pried off my feet. My spine tingled with alcohol and the thought of the one person I could count on—knowing it was the most dangerous thing in the world.

15

I awoke early, about ten o'clock, and paced around my house. I took a quick shower, leaving my phone on the bathroom counter in case he called. I put on makeup and dried my hair. When he still didn't call by twelve, I chain smoked my remaining cigarettes, blowing the smoke into the cold, stale air. I couldn't afford to turn on the heat unless it was crucial. I normally just wore layers and became so used to it that it rarely bothered me anymore. He finally called at one thirty.

"I have some bad news," he said.

"Yes?"

"Well, the guys have been bugging me and I have to hang out with them. Sorry."

"Oh," I said. He promised, said he would love nothing more than to hang out with me. Fuck Adam.

"Sure, whatever. Can we hang out before that? Or after that? Or today at all?"

"I guess I can pick you up for a bit before. But it can't be for very long."

"Yeah, sure," I answered, covering my disappointment. "You know where I live."

I know you are not my right
But why give up the fight
It's going to be a long fucking night

I got in his car and just stared straight out the windshield. He was ditching me for his friends. I wasn't really in the mood to talk at all. If only I had a flask or something. Then I wouldn't need him. I wouldn't need anything.

He turned the car into a parking lot and looked at me, trying to find some words of consolation for his jackass actions.

"What?" I asked.

"Nothing. You're just beautiful."

Beauty. No one looked on the inside where it really mattered.

Nobody saw who I was. They saw my "shining eyes", "pretty face", "perfect body". I was sick of it. The same compliments from every guy who just wanted an easy bang in the school parking lot. "Nice ass", "wicked eyes", "cute nose". Intelligent? Funny? I wanted someone to see that, but who was left to care?

"I'm sorry about today," he offered, "I really am."

"Okay."

"Don't be mad at me? Is there anything I can get you?" he said, ready to drop me off and go see his friends.

"How about a flask?"

"Sure thing."

He'd be fine with me walking around by myself with a flask. That showed how much he loved me. I thought of the party, when he said he would help me. I thought he said he'd rather just "chill out and watch a movie."

We pulled into the liquor store parking lot. Déjà vu. How many times had I done this, and how many more times would I in my lifetime? It was like an annoying top forty song that played over and over in your head despite your distaste for it. I was so sick of hearing it. I lit a cigarette.

"Buy me a pack of smokes, too!" I yelled out the window.

I sat in the car and waited for some sort of sign from the universe, to give me direction. I counted the cars in the parking lot, praying they would all spontaneously combust right then and there and take me with them. A kid and her father walked by, hand in hand. She had blonde hair, nice new clothes, and a fall jacket. She would be the cheerleader, the pretty girl. The girl that would fuck me up because I would never be that way. The father stared at me. He probably saw the fate of his own little girl in my young face, as I smoked a cigarette with my dirty, paint-stained hands. He furrowed his brow at the beating bass line.

It was a Sunday afternoon. All of the happy families would just be getting out of church and going home to their perfect houses for a home-cooked Sunday dinner. There was no God, no heaven. They just needed something to fall back on if everything fell apart. Didn't everyone? What did I have? A bottle, a few cigarettes.

Adam walked out of the liquor store. The brown bag with the key in a red circle and a diagonal line going through, it was more familiar to me than my own face. Don't drink and drive. It should have been a picture of a broken heart and a liquor bottle, with a warning to not let this fucking bullshit ruin your life.

Adam opened the door and passed me the flask. I downed a quarter of it before he even sat down. He drove around to the back of the parking lot and stopped the car. I recognized the brick wall from where we had been last night, the fast-food bag still strewn on the pavement.

"Well, I got a go," he stated, as if he were telling me he had to run to the bank or the store. Instead, he was ditching his fucked-up girlfriend with a bottle of liquor.

"Sure," I got out of the car and slammed the door. I should have given him the finger, or told him to not come back, or at least made an angry gesture, but I was too upset to muster the energy.

I wandered around the plaza, behind the liquor store, the sub shop, the dive bar—all the landmarks of my drunken life. I went to the coffee shop and poured two fingers of my flask in a coffee and sipped on it as I drew. I sketched myself on a bridge, arms opened to the sky. I drew bleeding eyes in trees, their branches descending like claws. I took every feeling and made it into art.

After I left the coffee shop, I sat behind the gas station and smoked. I let the images in front of me appear on my paper, my hands becoming red and purple, exposed in the cold air. The chain-link fence, the propane tanks for the gas station, the desolate clouds in the overcast sky. Time didn't exist. There was only me, my drawings.

The sky darkened, melting away the terrible day to become an even worse night. I didn't think about Adam. I didn't want to face the truth, the idea that I'd made a wrong decision.

If I get through this without being weak
Surely it will be a feat
I could have had a better situation
But, of course, there are always stipulations

At around seven, I went to the fast-food place to get the same shitty food Adam had ordered the other night. I was back to wasting all my money on bullshit.

I sat down with my food tray and made drunken conversation with the other patrons around me. I loved how I could talk and not care, not have a thing to worry about. I didn't have to repeat and alter my sentences in my head before I spoke, to make sure I didn't say something stupid. I didn't care what people thought right then. I didn't have to hide. I numbly ate my food and watched the clock. I went outside, leaving the tray and the ridiculous amount of garbage that came with a four-dollar meal. I lit a cigarette, and Adam's car turned into the parking lot. He rolled down the window.

"Get in," he instructed.

I stumbled into the car and started to laugh.

"What's up?" I asked.

"Not much, not much, not much. How are you?" he replied in his stoned-out bass. The red eyes revealed the damage of whatever he had done. I never asked.

"I am fucking wicked," synonymous for too drunk to care.

"You are loaded!" he exclaimed.

"Sure thing," I held up the flask that had not even a shot left. I was so cold though, it felt as if I were freezing from the inside out.

Adam accelerated out of the parking lot so fast my body flew back into the seat. I never had a chance to put on my seatbelt.

He charged up the main road, flying between cars, stoned-driving like he was in some sort of video game world where everything was fun and fantasy. I laughed as safe drivers with kids in car seats honked their horns in disbelief. Maybe things weren't so bad after all. He looked at me and laughed.

I didn't talk, just chain-smoked, watched the houses and trees blur past the window. The music pumped through my body, and vibrated the car. A car pulled up beside us. A bunch of Adam's friends hung out the window, yelling over their loud music that competed with ours. Jeremy and Jordan had their windows rolled down, and I recognized a couple of the other guys from the party.

"Pull over!" Jeremy yelled, gesturing wildly towards the shoulder of the road.

They drove alongside us for a few more seconds, until we found somewhere semi-safe to pull over. Jeremy jumped out of the car and the other guys called things at me through the window.

"Hey sexy!" one of them yelled at me, turning to his friends and laughing. I smiled confidently and winked.

Jeremy got in Adam's backseat. I sized him up through the rear-view mirror. His blonde hair came down over his left eye on a vicarious angle, the rest was perfectly straight and landed at the back of his neck. He was wearing an orange leather jacket that was fully open, with no shirt on underneath. He was so slim. I could see his abs and his smooth skin. Although he looked like he would sound high-pitched and whiny, his voice was low and husky.

"Hey there," he said, patting me on the shoulder from behind, "what up?"

"Hey," I replied, "we met at Adam's party, you probably don't remember." I cringed at the thought of that night.

"Oh yeah, yeah. You're the one taking up all Adam's time," he punched Adam in the shoulder and they had a fake fight. "Just kidding man. You're pretty cool, I suppose."

"Thanks," I added, "I always wanted to be pretty cool. Although that's not a very descriptive adjective."

Jeremy reached into his pocket to retrieve a large bag of weed. Adam turned on the inner car light so they could both see what they were doing.

"How much man?" Jeremy asked Adam.

"Well, I got a hundred and fifty bucks, but you better cut me a deal. The last shit you gave me was bunk."

"Ahh man, you're running me dry."

"Come on now," Adam replied with a hint of irony, "who got you all those deals this week?"

"Whatever man," Jeremy said, taking another bag from his pocket, "help me get rid of these, then."

Jeremy passed a little bag to Adam. It had numerous pills of various colours in it. Adam held it to the light and shook it around a little.

"Twenty percent," Adam said, as he laid the baggie in the glove compartment.

Jeremy rolled his eyes and then spun up a joint. Adam used the power button to put all the windows down so we could converse with his other friends in the car parked next to us.

"I hear you like this stuff?" one of the guys said to me, holding up an unopened mini-flask. He had wildly curly hair and a face with strangely misplaced features. He passed it to me from his backseat. I reached out the window to grab it. It was a dark rum. I opened it and drank half of it, passed it back.

"I'm Lily," I said as he drank the remainder.

"Kevin," he said, spitting out the window.

"We are in the same science class," I added.

"Oh yeah, I'm never there."

"Me neither," I said, and we laughed.

Jeremy lit up the joint and took a long drag and passed it to Adam. Adam took a hit, and it made its way to me. What the hell, I thought as I smoked it. Once the joint had travelled between both of the cars, all the guys got out and hung out in a big circle. They smoked cigarettes and laughed at their own popular celebrity impersonations. I stayed in my seat, my head pounding, my body too tired to move an inch.

I reflected on many things sitting in that cold seat, lighting smoke after smoke, and ignoring the loud laughter. I was no longer a child, and I knew no one else would look out for me. I realized there were two very distinct options. I could be strong and survive, make a real life for myself, or let myself fall into this abyss and get crushed. I started making a plan.

At least I had my uncle. I knew he would take me in at any moment, he had told me many times. I decided to do it on my own. I was working full-time, and in a few weeks I would have enough for a ticket. I could finish school out there, find a new job, try to pay him rent, which I knew he wouldn't accept.

I should have thought of it sooner. He had no children and he always thought of me as his daughter. He still called every Sunday, and I did as I always did, and pretended everything was great. I know it was hard for the both of us that we had no idea where my mother was.

I formulated my plan—I would not spend a dime these next two weeks so I could buy a ticket. I reached into the console when no one was looking and took the baggie of pills. I could use a little pocket money.

When my dad was gone, on a school day, I would pack my most important things and just get a cab to the airport. It would be so simple. I made a vow to call my uncle in the next few days and let him know when he could pick me up. I wasn't going to let the world crush me. I had learned enough to know that no one else could live my life for me, and I just wasn't going to survive at the rate I was going. It wasn't a brave escape like the street kids, but at least it was something to keep me alive.

I felt a weight lift off of my soul. I could escape this. I could change things. I didn't even care about Adam and his whiny friends. I was leaving anyway, nothing I did here anymore mattered. I got out of the car.

"Do any of you know who Freud is?" I asked. They all stopped what they were doing and stared at me blankly. I laughed and laughed.

"Didn't think so," I added, turning back to the car. I turned around. "And by the way Adam, you were the one who picked me up, so I am ready to go home now. Later, dudes."

Adam drove me back home, puzzled at my sudden change in personality. Turned out all I needed was something to look forward to. I sang along softly to the radio, refusing Adam's offer to smoke a joint. I interlocked my hands with each other so he couldn't hold them, and I rested them on my lap instead.

As he pulled in my driveway, I looked at him and said, "That was really shitty to ditch me today. How about I call you if I want to hang?"

I didn't give him a chance to answer, just shut the door and pretty much skipped to my door. I turned the heat up as far as it would go, I got a bubble bath and used the good soap. When I got out, I stole the blanket and sheets off my dad's uninhabited bed and tucked them onto my small twin mattress. I turned the radio to the classical station, lit some incense and looked forward to tomorrow.

16

The next few days were easy. I was so excited about my plan, writing details out in my notebook and washing my clothes to be packed, that I didn't have the time to worry. Between planning, school and working, I didn't even take the time out to drink. I ran out of cigarettes for a whole day without even realizing it.

I knew I was only leaving anyway, so even school was entertaining. I said anything, I did anything. I spoke up in class and gave intelligent monologues about our latest English book. I was the first one to raise my hand in science class, and even got a perfect score on a math test. I noticed a lot of people raising their eyebrows at my full-day attendance, and my attentiveness in class. I floated around, adding my own two cents to the conversations.

I never called Adam once. Sure, I thought about it, but why make it worse on him? I knew he wouldn't give a shit either way. It was my turn to ditch him. Luckily, in the next few weeks, I got my work to jack up my hours. Every day after school I had an hour to get to work, and by the time I got home I just wanted to shower and go to bed.

I didn't think I was capable of feeling so free, yet there I was. I was writing giant lists of things I was going to do in the next few months— writing songs, poems, painting and drawing. I felt like the energy was endless. I could talk as fast as an auctioneer until someone told me they could barely understand what I was saying. I served more customers at work than anyone else who was working, flying from one to the next at lightning speed.

I even got up at five a.m. to jog around the trail by the river before school, despite the frost on the ground and the world turning to winter.

I tried calling my uncle a few times but there was no answer at his house. I didn't think anything of it—he had no kids or wife. He was a construction worker who had long hours during certain months, and none the next. If he wasn't home, he was probably working or hanging out at the casino. I had his address, from the card he had sent me for my birthday, so I had no worry that I wouldn't find him.

Everything was going to be so easy from now on. I felt a future, I gripped on to something that wasn't just in my imagination, and it was something I could truly hold on to. Graduating high school, maybe even college. Food in the fridge. The good kind of soap that left you clean instead of feeling even dirtier. Living by my own will. Only myself that I needed. This time it was going to work perfectly.

I was in my living room, painting an abstract sunset. Incense rose to the ceiling in clouds, while Etta James whispered candy words into my ear. There was a knock on the door. I knew it would only be a matter of time before Adam would show up on my doorstep, begging for forgiveness. I pictured him with sad looking flowers drooping in his hand, heard him declaring his love for me.

I let him knock again a few minutes more. I happily added more dapples of colour before I rose to open the door. I had been planning this very moment for many days now, the moment I would see the look of disappointment on his stupid face when I rejected him.

By the time I reached the dilapidated porch, however, I knew from the blurred image behind the frosted glass that it was definitely not Adam. He stood half a foot taller, wore a hat. An immediate sense of dread filled the day. I had no idea who it was. I paused while I debated whether or not I should open the door, but then remembered that it was me, that it was our family, our house everybody was scared of. If anyone tried to fuck around, I would just remind them who my father was.

"Who's there?" I asked, before I made the final step to unlocking the door.

"Good afternoon. I am Detective Norman. I am here to see S. Myles."

Detective Norman? Now I started to feel the fear. The dread that you feel when you know that someone is about to burst your happy little bubble so fast that you will have to scrambled to pick up the pieces. Had someone found out that it was me who put the six-foot anarchy symbol on the side of the school in orange spray paint? Did I kick the shit out of some rich little bastard while I was loaded and forgot I had done so, the "detective", their father, coming to put me in my place? Or the last, most shocking option. He was here for my father. It was over. The drugs, the parties. The child abuse.

I slowly turned the lock and opened the door. Detective Norman was younger than I thought he would be. He looked thoughtful in his blue uniform. The goatee under his chin suggested maybe he did read books and drink herbal tea on his day off. Or maybe he just had a good radar for the latest trends.

After a few awkward moments, I remembered that he had asked if my father was home. I realized I had been holding my breath.

"That's my father. He is not home right now," I answered, ready to defend him, prepared to lie. I knew how to fight for the household, too. I had been taught by the best.

Detective Norman put his head down to consult his notes, maybe to make a call on his police radio, maybe to alert the authorities.

"Do you know when he will be arriving home?" he asked with a newer tone in his voice, maybe one of sympathy. Pity, probably.

"I don't know," I answered truthfully. I knew the Detective would have no trouble believing it. "I don't get to see him a lot on the weekdays. I work full-time and we are on different schedules."

As I looked into Detective Norman's pale blue eyes, the kindness they held, I knew this was going to be less about me and more about something that would fuck me up forever. Just in the way he held himself. Of course, men made it seem a lot easier, they covered up pain with clearing their throats or looking important, both of which this detective did at that moment.

"And you are the only other adult in the household?"

Adult. Full-time job. Lines around the eyes.

"Yes, it is just myself and my father here."

He tipped his hat, licked his lips.

"You might want to sit down."

I poured boiling water into his mug, and the water turned the murky colour of tea. I placed it in front of him with a small jug of milk. I found a teaspoon and even a little jar of sugar.

"Thanks a lot," Detective Norman said to me as he took a sip of his tea, "you really didn't have to do that."

"Sure I did. As long as you are a guest in my home you will be treated as one." I enjoyed talking to adults, acting like one. I watched Norman's eyes take in the room around him—the incense burner, the almost finished oil painting. I was grateful I'd spent the last few days doing one final cleanup of the desolate house before I said goodbye. It looked better than it had in years. Probably even better than it ever had.

"I'm ready for whatever it is you have to tell me," I said to him, matter-of-factly. I made my voice sound as if I actually believed those words myself.

"This is going to be very hard," he said.

"I know. I knew you weren't here with Girl Guide Cookies." I laughed—my feeble attempt at keeping the air light. Norman seemed to know that, as if he were used to telling people their lives were about to fall apart.

He looked down at his notes one final time, and bit the inside of his cheek. I could see the indent he made, and that he bit hard.

"Well," he started, not sure where to go from there, "there has been a tragedy." He stopped then, and I could see him rehearsing this exact speech in the rear-view mirror on his drive here. It was like his whole life had been lived just to exist at this moment where he could tell me what he needed to say.

"It seems the interprovincial police departments have been trying to track down some of your family members for about a week now. The province where your mother is listed as residing contacted us. Unfortunately, she could not be located, but, as I am sure you know, is thought to be alive." He said this last bit carefully, as if I wasn't already aware of the fact that my mother was on the run, that she was a dumb fucking crack addict. That I probably wouldn't ever see her again.

"Go on," I edged him on in a small quiet voice. If it wasn't my mother dead, which wouldn't surprise me, then I had no idea what to expect.

"Well, when the police department failed to locate your mother, they contacted us here to get in contact with your father." He paused, as if that statement would have any significance for me. He continued on after taking a breath. "Well, according to the file they faxed down to us, and I am going to tell you this first but will have to return to officially alert your father, he was listed as the next of kin. And since you are his daughter, you have the right to know, legally speaking."

"Okay," I replied, "someone has passed away, and that is horrible, however I am not close to any of my relatives, and I am not totally sure who you are referring to."

"Well, based on this information, the man William Harris is listed as your uncle, he was found last week in his vehicle near his home. According to the autopsy results, it was due to a drug overdose. It has been ruled as a suicide. I am very sorry."

My uncle. The world stopped. Him. William. Willie. Bill. Uncie B. Everything. Fucking. Ruined. Suicide. Drug overdose. My Plan. My fucking only family. My fucking uncle killed himself. Dead. Alone. Suicide. A week. I tuned everything out, the detective was not there, I was not even there. The house, the world, it disappeared. I became someone else entirely.

Sitting in a yellow room. Sitting on the lap of a man who smelled like tobacco, laughing at my footie pyjamas. My mom laughing along through the partition while she was in the kitchen, buttering toast. A hug, a warm body. Feeling safe. Never, ever being able to return to it. I felt my whole life disappear. I was once again nothing. Destined for nothing. A soulless body.

I didn't even realize that Norman was still sitting at my kitchen table. I was somewhere else entirely. He kept talking, I couldn't understand a word he was saying, as if cotton had been stuffed in my ears, as if my mouth was gag tied. I couldn't speak. I couldn't think. I couldn't breathe. I hoped I would just die then, too.

What if I got to the phone? What if I had left a fucking week earlier? What if I sent an email, a card? What if I called the police when I couldn't get hold of him? What if I had been more connected to him? Why didn't I just know that something was wrong? Why didn't I know he died? Why couldn't I hear him calling for help? Why was I so selfish? Why wasn't it just me instead?

I was dimly aware of Norman leaving his card and some papers on my table, heard a door close. I don't know how long I sat there. It was definitely hours—the sky was dark before I realized I was still a person.

I couldn't cry. That's probably the weirdest thing. I couldn't let myself feel pain. There is no word to describe it. It was pure emptiness. Unanimated. Liquidated. Spiritless.

It's a battle to hold on
Milk carton faces that dared to dream
Wounded and falling apart at the seams
When there is nowhere left to go
There is no place to call home
This will never leave me, nor I, It
It is somewhere I will have to exist

Reluctantly, with numb fingers, I called the first person I could think of.

17

I got into Adam's car and hunched down into the seat. He looked surprised to see me, and I didn't blame him, but at that time I couldn't care about anyone else's feelings except for my own. No one mattered anymore. I was done with everybody, indefinitely.

"So…?" he asked.

"So," I said back, "my uncle just fucking killed himself. So, drive. To the liquor store. I don't think I want to talk yet."

Adam changed the gear shift into drive, I lit up a smoke that was in his console and blew smoke into the car, didn't bother to waste my energy on opening the window. I flipped through my CD case to an unmarked CD someone had once made of all my favourite songs. I turned the volume all the way up and let the screeching guitar solos and heavy bass settle deep inside of me.

In this river all will fade to black,
In this river ain't no coming back.

Although I had thought I'd already been there for the last time, Adam pulled into the shuddersome parking lot of the liquor store.

"What do you want?" he asked me.

I threw him a twenty from my wallet. I wouldn't be needing any of my money after all. Might as well waste what I had saved on alcohol and drugs.

"Big bottle of fucking scotch. That's what he drank. Yeah. Scotch." I stopped talking to look at myself in the mirror, the dead eyes, the limp hair, the nothingness of it all. "Pack of smokes too," I added. I was thoughtless, I had no more words. They were in the grave with him now.

After Adam got back into the car, I downed the bottle of scotch straight, smoked cigarettes one after another until Adam had to drive to a store to get me more, which I paid for myself.

There was alcohol, there was weed, and there was blow. There was Jeremy and Jordan, another few guys I didn't know, or maybe I did, I just didn't care. We were parked in the woods next to a river. I looked at it rage, and could have easily just fallen into it.

In this river ain't no coming back.

There were a lot of times I got fucked up, passed out on floors, on the ground, in the car. Whatever it was tonight, I just kept going. Maybe it was the shock of it all. I drank vodka from a bottle, warm beers in cans, red and white wine straight from the bottle. Joint after joint—I wasn't even sure what was in them anymore. My mind was a cacophony of drugs. Nothing else.

I can recall at one point, Jordan looked at me and said, "Sorry, bros before hoes man."

I tried to argue with him, telling him I was a bro and not a ho. It only made them laugh more.

I really don't know much from here. Like I said, it all fell together into one long, wasted day. I'm not sure how I got home that night, if I even went home, or how long we, or I, spent drinking by the river. I feel as if it were multiple days. I have a memory that I watched the sunrise and sunset at least a couple of times. I didn't sleep. It was the biggest binge I had ever been on.

Inevitably, my father found out about his brother-in-law's suicide, and he withdrew even more. I don't remember if I went to school or not, I didn't care. Every now and then I could smell marijuana floating from the basement, and hear the sound of shitty classic rock, and old drunks arguing. I didn't, or maybe I couldn't, pay attention to it anymore. I was done with him, too.

In the endless cold nights, I often hung out with Adam. He drove his car down the frosty roads, I sipped from a flask. A party here, a bar there. In his bed, in his car.

As toxic as Adam was for me, I kept going back for more. That was who I was and there are only a few events I even remember. Everything was drunk or stoned or just generally disassociated. What I do remember has never left me.

18

December. The worst month for the lonely. That bottomless feeling of desperation. Adam stuck by me, and we went out. I pretended to enjoy myself, searching for the first second that I could make an excuse to have a drink.

On nights Adam was working, I just walked in the cold by myself, trying to forget. I would always end up with beer, on a trail, sitting on a rock, on a bridge. Screaming into the night. Screaming at him. Screaming and crying at everything—the hopelessness, the knowledge I could never be a normal person now, not after that.

I was starting to come around to more of myself a few weeks before Christmas. I knew deep inside that my uncle wouldn't have wanted me to wallow in a pitiful heartache for the rest of time. I managed to brush my hair, I read a book.

I was waiting for Adam one morning. He had called me and said he was taking me to the city to watch the Christmas parade. I was not from one of those proper families that went to Christmas parades, that drink hot chocolate, and go to church on Sundays. As late as it was for me to relive a childhood fantasy of watching crappy homemade floats of Santa and reindeers, I found myself feeling excited.

It was a sunny winter day. Uncle William was dead and I stopped wondering why for once. My dad had stopped bothering me like I was some sort of maid. I had the feeling, the first in such a long time, that today was going to be a good day.

Adam was to get me at ten a.m., and the parade was to start by noon. He knew you had to leave early to get a parking spot, and just where to go and when to do things. I hoped that one day I would be that kind of person. As I paced my house, peeking through the ratty curtains every five minutes, checking the clock obsessively, ten o'clock came and went. So did eleven. Thinking he was just running late, I called his house. His brother told me he had left about an hour ago.

Then I worried. If a schedule was not working as planned, my mind always went straight to the worst things. Car accident. Seizure. I talked myself out of my miserable anxieties—I was not going to let anything ruin my first decent day. I figured he had probably just stopped for smokes and coffee, or maybe he drove to Jeremy's for some marijuana.

Then noon came and went as well. I sat on the couch and stared at the wall. I picked up my pack of smokes with my shaking hands and lit one after the other. It was too cold to open a window and the smoke filled the house. I flipped through a book of inspirational quotes my uncle had sent me, trying so hard to find just one positive thing to hang on to. I cried. I threw my phone at the wall. I called Adam. I checked the window. I walked to the end of the street. I checked my email.

Then it was dark. I left my house, went into the freezing night, and I walked. I didn't look back. I walked until morning. I vowed to never get excited about anything ever again.

When I got home early in the morning, I sat in my backyard and finished off my pack of smokes. I watched my hot breath turn into steam in the cold winter air. When I finally went inside, I picked up the bottle of vodka that I knew was half filled with water. I poured as much as I could into a glass, and drank until it was gone.

Around noon I was already plastered, and running on absolutely no sleep, which seemed to intensify my inebriation. I heard my computer make the intrusive sound for a new email. I immediately let out a breath I didn't know I had been holding. I prayed it was Adam with an explanation.

"Hey, I was talking to some of the guys and I don't think we should see each other anymore. I'll drop off your CDs. Bye."

I don't remember replying to Adam but inevitably I did. What I wrote didn't make much sense.

"First of ALL ADAM, u ditched me yesterday. Like I am just a fish in the bowl, u are my fish too. I see who you are, I see you more than your stupid stoner friends. I know that you need me and you are just being naïve in listening to them. I will wait till you come around because I know this is not you talking. Listen to me I am meant 2 figure it all out and so u should know this is serious. I make the choices now so 2 bad 4 u. Everything will be fine with us. Everything will work out."

For some reason, I attached a picture of the *Mona Lisa* I had saved from the internet.

"Adam, this is a work of art. Look at her sad eyes. This is me. You can't just do this. I know this is not you. I can't believe how mean you are being. This is irrational. You are being irrational. You can't just leave me alone with all this. I can change I swear. Your friends are fucking idiots. You are kind of a fucking idiot yourself as well. I am sorry, you are just being an idiot. Ok please call me! Don't leave me here. It is a rock, your soul. I can fix it. I can fix it. Please don't do this."

It always goes back to the beginning
At what point do I stop trying
Is it nature or nurture to blame
Do you blame the whole link or just the chain

You take a hit and I will take a sip
Fuck this, it is all an act

I finally managed to fall asleep. I woke up around dinner time with a hangover. That's probably the saddest feeling, waking up and realizing it's dark outside and you are still slightly drunk from the morning. The first thing I did was ravage the cupboards for more alcohol. I found a half bottle of rum behind the dusty pots and pans. I didn't even bother with a glass this time, just drank straight from the bottle.

I don't remember leaving my house. I can't recall how drunk I actually was, I just remember that I was back to where it started. Down the trail, past the bridge, behind the pub and the sub shop. In a parking lot of cars. No teenagers tonight, it must have been one of those sad evenings like Monday or Tuesday where nothing actually happens, as if people are afraid to have fun on the weekdays.

I looked in every car, thinking I would see Adam. As if being here would just take me back to that night when I had met him, when I felt I could start over. It wasn't even a question of if I would change anything, it was just a fact that I would change everything if I could. I wished I could just start right from the beginning, or go back to just being a peanut sized fetus and say, "fuck this." Get out while I still had the chance.

As I stumbled between the cars, there was a group of people with their windows rolled down. They were in front of the fast-food place, smoking a joint. For reasons I can't really explain, I decided to speak with an accent, to pretend I was from Germany.

"Heylo there, may I have zome of that?"

They turned to look at me as I peeked in the driver side window—a skinny man with blonde curly hair in his mid-twenties, a large guy in the passenger seat, a plain looking girl in the back wearing a colourful hat. I knew I had never met them before, and they were definitely too old to be in my school.

"Where you from anyways?" the blonde guy asked me.

"I am from Germany. I visit my uncle here but I went to the bar, I am not sure how to get home now. Maybe you help?"

"Sure, get in! We love company!"

I got into the back seat next to the girl, shook her hand and smiled. They eyed me as they passed me the joint and I took a puff.

"I never met anyone from Germany before, what's it like?" the girl asked me.

"It so good," I replied as I exhaled through my nose, "so much art and music. Not like here, nothing to do. I am bored, I know only my uncle. He work on the fishing boat and his boss live here, so I visit him now."

They all seemed impressed by meeting someone in that small town who actually had some cultural experience. Real or not, they did not know the difference.

"So how old are you?" the larger guy asked me.

"Oh, I am twenty-seven," I replied in my accent.

"Wow," the blonde guy said, "I am Kirk, and I am twenty-two, this is my cousin Greg, and he is twenty-five, and my girlfriend there…"

"Kayla," she stated, shaking my hand again, "so good to meet you?"

"Simone," I said, without pausing.

"So," Greg asked, turning up the music, "do you have a lot of weed in Germany?"

Everyone laughed.

"Oh yes," I replied. "Much better than this, though. Your weed like straw. Germany weed is better. No chemicals."

"Well, maybe next time you visit you can bring us some."

"Sure, and thank you for sharing with me. Nothing to do here."

"So," Greg said again, "do you like music?"

"Oh, of course. I love music. I like Wagner, and Rammstein is very good. Lots of metal in Germany. Metal capital of the world! But I enjoy classical much more."

Kirk lit up a smoke and held out his pack to me. I took one, lit it with the lighter that followed. I told them so much bullshit sitting in that car. About my apartment in some made up city, the university, how the men never washed their pants. Whatever I came up with they bought, and the more shit I made up, the happier I felt.

We sat in the car for a few hours, talking about our lives. I expressed interest in the lifestyle of living in a small town in the middle of nowhere, they asked me questions about Germany. I felt as if I had made some friends that I would be willing to see again, although I was "flying home" in a couple of days.

When we were all extremely high, Kirk started up the car and said he would give me a ride home. Without thinking, I told him the name of a street. It was Adam's street.

"I know exactly where that is," he said. "We will get you home all safe."

That one simple sentence made me want to weep. Sometimes someone can just say the simplest thing and it seems to touch a place that no one has ever found. No, I wouldn't be going home, wherever that was. And no, safe was not what I would be that night.

After refusing to be let out at the door (German tradition), I got out at the end of the street. They all expressed how great it was to meet me. I did the same. I really did have a great time and appreciated having free smokes and weed, and somewhere warm to sit for a little while.

Kirk handed me a few cigarettes and I gratefully accepted them. I scrawled a fake foreign email onto a page of his notebook. I said goodbye and walked away, watched the car drive off into the distance. I looked ahead at Adam's road, all those suburban houses, the dark woods. All those nightmares in disguise.

It must have been the middle of the night. I peered down the street to Adam's house, one forlorn porch light the only nearby source of light. I snuck behind his house and made myself comfortable on a large rock in his backyard.

My hands were turning purple. I lit up another smoke, shaking as I brought it to my mouth. Realizing I couldn't just sit there in his backyard all night, I worked up the courage to use the return of my CDs as an excuse to knock on his door.

I stumbled up the small hill and onto his driveway, made my way to the basement door, where he and his brother had an "apartment." One of those places where you don't have to pay rent and mom still picks your socks up off the floor.

I stood in front of his door for about five minutes until I decided to knock. I waited another few minutes, and knocked again, a bit harder this time. Nobody answered. I knocked harder, then pounded the door at minute intervals. Eventually, Adam's brother answered the door in his boxers.

"What do you want?" he asked, "It's three a.m."

"I'm here for my CDs," I answered confidently. "Adam said he would bring them to me but he didn't and I really need them."

"At three a.m.?" he said again, groggily.

"Yes. I do. I work night shifts, so I am up late. Sorry if your lifestyle is a little more traditional. Now, can you get Adam for me?"

He shut the door in my face with a mumble along the lines of "be right back." I laughed to myself at how mad I had made him. I only hoped I could get to Adam that much. I saw his brother's face behind the door once again.

"He is in bed," Adam's brother informed me.

"Well, that's unfortunate," I replied, "because I am not, and he said he was going to do something and he didn't, and it's his own fault he fucked it up. Now, he can goddamn well get up for thirty seconds to give back my CDs. They are the only thing I care about and I am not letting that motherfucker take anything else from me."

His brother stared at me in bewilderment and didn't say anything else.

"So, go on," I gestured, "it's a simple fucking task. Thanks."

He shut the door once again and reappeared in about five minutes.

"He doesn't want to talk to you. I am sorry."

"Well, that's really too bad. Do I have to get the CDs myself? I am not scared of any of you. It's not that hard to break a window."

He just stared back at me. I kept my fiery gaze fixed on him.

"Okay, I'll be back." He shut the door once again and I stood there for another five minutes. I could hear them talking inside. He came back to the door, no Adam or CD case in sight.

"He really doesn't want to talk to you," he told me sympathetically, rubbing his eyes.

"Perfect," I replied. "I am not looking for a fucking conversation. How hard is it to get me my fucking CDs? Okay, it's not a big fucking shit show, just get my CD case and I will be on my way. Or I can come back at noon when no one is home, get the key from under the mat, and help myself to some of the money in the china cabinet as well. Which do you prefer?"

"You really need to leave," he told me shakily.

"I don't need anything except my goddam CDs!"

"Listen, he doesn't want to see you. Go away. Or I will call the police."

"Oh yes, I am sure the police will just have nothing better to do."

He slammed the door, but I wasn't giving up. I pounded on it for another five minutes until I saw Adam running to the door with no shirt on. He opened the door an inch, threw my CD case into the driveway, and locked the door in one quick motion, leaving me standing there.

"Thanks, you piece of shit!" I yelled at his house. "This isn't over! Guess you can't read—nobody fucks with me! Nobody fucks with me!"

I then sped off back toward the trail and plunked myself back onto the rock. I slowly enjoyed the last cigarette that Kirk had given me. Then, I remembered the baggie of pills I had stolen from Adam's car. I had been too fucked in my own head to even think about selling them. In fact, I had forgotten about them. I dug them out of my bag.

There were about fifteen pills in the bag, but I only took five, one of each colour. I had no idea what they were. Within fifteen minutes I was high as a kite, riding the elevator into the sky, a being meant to fly.

I laughed. I forgot about Adam and his bullshit attitude. I was in awe of the sound of my footsteps echoing into the night sky, the way my movements seemed to have a time lapse. When I waved my hands in front of my face, they lingered before my eyes, even after I had them by my sides. I laughed at everything. The dead sky, the darkness, the water rushing under the bridge. The tears on my face that were real or imagined, I couldn't tell. Everything was real, nothing was real.

This would be the key to my existence, to consume any sort of drug that could make me leave my own head for even one second of aerial bliss. I recognized a light in the distance—an all-night gas bar across the road from one of the trail entrances. There was a forlorn looking young man behind the counter. His nose piercing glinted from the fluorescent lights, and his tattoos were mismatched with his polo shirt uniform. I needed a friend, and maybe he did, too. I definitely needed cigarettes.

"Hey!" I exclaimed as I stumbled into the store.

"Hello," he replied, somewhat bemused. He was probably used to slews of drunk people coming into the store for cigarettes or old hot dogs.

"So," I said leaning on to the counter with my elbows, "I would like a pack of Marlboro Kings please."

"Do you have ID?" he smiled.

"Yes," I answered, "I usually do. But not right now."

"Well," he said," I can't sell you cigarettes. I could get in shit for that man."

"Nobody else is here. I swear I am twenty-one. See, I just broke up with my boyfriend, my ID is in his car, he wouldn't give it back because he is such a cocksucker. So, I am out of smokes and I am pissed. Please."

"I am sorry for your troubles, really," he added, "but I can't break the law."

I was on the brink of tears. I didn't really realize until then that it was always Adam who bought my cigarettes for me. I couldn't even have a goddamn cigarette.

"He is such a motherfucker," I exclaimed, "I had to argue to get my CDs back." I took the case from my bag and opened it up, flipped through the wallet. "They are all here, then. Except Nickelback. That's perfectly fine with me."

The store guy laughed. I was happy he understood my joke.

"Well, that's good."

"Yeah. I just don't understand why it's so hard to give somebody back their own belongings. What a fucker."

"Sounds like you're better off." He was attempting to cheer me up. I obviously needed it.

"Wanna buy some pills?" I asked him. He raised his eyebrow. "I mean, my boyfriend stole all my money, so I stole his stash. I really could use the money."

"I don't do that stuff, man," he told me.

I looked down at the counter, eyed up all the lotto tickets protected in their precious glass case. Everything seemed really strange to me, my high was turning to paranoia. I almost wished there was a pill I could take to stop being high. I felt like I was going to be sick, I felt like I was turning around in circles.

"You know what?" the guy asked, "I can't sell you smokes from here but it seems like you could use a bit of a break tonight."

I looked at him gratefully with what felt like half-closed eyes.

"If you meet me out back for my break, I can give you some of mine. How about that?"

"That would be awesome, man," I answered with a smile, "thank you so much."

I started to get my CDs into my bag when I fell off the world. Everything just turned into an incomprehensible swirl of colours, my brain a liquefied montage of memories, the ceiling. The floor. The faint words of the store clerk, a language I no longer knew. The fear. The relief. And then, nothing.

I wait in limbo
For the morning light to set it
I can finally open my eyes
Shut this book
Write another chapter
Let myself be free a little faster

19

Everyone came to my funeral. It was quite the spectacle—the colourful flowers against the falling snow, my friends huddled in front my casket, leaning into each other and crying. They even closed the school for the day.

My father found out first. I watched him as he lit a joint, took a sip of beer, shaking with disbelief. I had felt like he didn't love me for so long, but I was the one that kept him going. From time to time, I would visit the house, watch him sleep. Even though he never did change, I also knew he could never recover. I no longer needed glimmers of hope. I was free.

People shared stories about how much they missed me. Chad, from the ice cream store, cried about how sweet I was. Even Allison remembered me playing guitar at the grade eight school talent show. Josh's eyes were still red. Everybody that ever knew me remembered something about me. I was finally noticed. It was the door I held open once, the note I left on a desk, the amazing paper I submitted. It was nothing specific, but it was all of the little things, the snippets of things from my existence that were important.

I followed my friends first. I started with Jessica, who loved me in death just as much as in life. She was so beautiful, and the fact I hurt her was the biggest pain. I tried to comfort her tears, but I was just a wisp of smoke. I could hear her reaching out to me, but we could never touch each other.

I was there for that wedding, though, and she had a thousand paper swans. I didn't make them, but I knew what it meant to her. She was the first person to visit my grave. She brought paper swans she'd made herself. They were poorly done, but I basked in her love and the fact that she had tried. She brought the swans to the baby shower, too. Even now she often smiles at our memories.

Dan was next. He found out about me through Jessica, while getting his decaf with two sugars. They shed a tear together. He didn't know in time for the funeral, but he sat at my grave and drank a dozen Budweiser, poured one out on my grave and cried. After he was plastered, he went to the bar. I watched as he sadly head-banged to the music that he chose on the jukebox, his hair flowing madly in the air. He did end up writing the book. He always leaves empty beer bottles on my grave—it's his version of flowers. I was his catalyst for change. Part of me had given him a sense of a future. Where I couldn't have it, he tried. It was time for him to try for himself.

I followed Josh briefly. He became a good father, the kind that he never had. I saw him push his kid on the swings, his eyes blue and no longer rimmed with crimson. He was always waiting to be saved and he finally realized that a saviour came wearing diapers, sometimes.

Katelyn visited me too, in her own way. She lit incense, and a cigarette, in the middle of the night. She called my name, tears streaming down her face, as she searched for answers. I was there, but I could never get through, only see. She never did get married. She followed in her mom's footsteps—the bars, the drugs, the partying. I hope she knows I am watching out for her.

The day after I died was a really weird day at school. No one said much. Girls whose names I never even knew went home sick and cried on their beds. The school planned a remembrance ceremony for me. It was even in the paper, and soon everyone would know.

The only thing I could do was watch from wherever I was stuck. I wasn't sure even where I was, just that I was in some sort of weird in-between world that most people never get to experience or talk about. In the most perverse way possible, I was lucky.

Everyone cried about me. The teachers wondered if there was something they could have done. I saw them sitting, looking out their windows, and thinking of me.

On other days, I would just watch anybody. I could be anywhere. People are fascinating to watch. Through them I got to experience everything I should have when I was alive. I would watch lovers whisper in each other's ears, and I started to learn what love was. I would watch the street kids. I used to want to be them. When they passed out drunk on their backpacks, they all wished they were home. They would look at the stars and pray for anyone to help them. I hoped they felt me watching over them.

Here there are no real people—we are just waiting for what's next. It's difficult to explain. We are not alive but we are not really dead, either. For all of the things that led up to my suicide, I wish I could walk amongst you.

Adam missed me, initially. But he was lucky to get out of the lifestyle he was living. He became a minister at his parents' church. It may have been guilt about me—he knows what he did.

I have seen everyone in their darkest moments. I have seen Jessica and her child leave flowers at my grave. I have watched Katelyn shoot up. I have seen Josh deal with a child with gastro. But I am also not stuck here. I have gotten to see the world that I always wanted. I have seen the New York streets, the buskers, the people singing their way home. I have been to Amsterdam for those smoking hot evenings. I can see everything I dreamt of, and still look into my hometown from time to time.

I simply exist in the molecules, a part of nature, a part of the sky. I am the star that you talk to when you're too afraid to cry. I am the grains of sand you let fall between your fingers. I am everywhere and nowhere. You have a chance. Take it and run. Your story is not over.

Acknowledgements

This has been a project almost twenty years in the making, so if you are reading this, then I thank you. Shout out to Tom for ordering me take-out and parenting our children while I was working through finishing this book. Thank you, Sheri, for feeding me and letting me sit on your couch and write; and for when I couldn't, thank you for making sure I left the house, and for talking me through so many things. I am lucky to have you.

To Krystahh for all the play dates and late-night chats after the kids were asleep; you are the vein of my support system and I love you dearly. To Maggie, even though you are far away, you will always answer my call—miles apart do not change inside jokes.

For everyone that provided child care so I could work on this project, you are so appreciated: Jen, Jade, Stella, Alyssa, Alycia, Hazel and Kaylah. To my dedicated and appreciated employees, who swear I don't overwork them, just know I appreciate you all taking on extra work while I wrote: Chanelle, Kayte, Angie, Kim, Sam, and Ashley, your work is never unnoticed, and I love you like family. For my late-night video chat pals—Andrea, Richard and Chris—you are my backbone.

This book would never have happened without my fabulous editor, JE Solo. You have restored my confidence in myself and your work is essential. Thank you the most.

And for Ozzy, Astrid and Cohen, the children that keep me alive. Stay Gold.

About the Author

Leslie Butt is an Indigenous Canadian, a mother of three, and an avid writer, painter, poet, musician and home renovator, depending on the day. She is the author of "Fifteen" and "Bring on the Dark." She is also the CEO of 709 Clean Team and the Operations Manager at THC Distribution.

She lives in Portugal Cove, Newfoundland with her children, and an absurd garden. Leslie looks forward to friends dropping by to help her water her plants, and discuss lucid dreams. She lives a quiet life full of gratitude and fullness, despite the resiliency that is required.

www.ingramcontent.com/pod-product-compliance
Lightning Source LLC
Chambersburg PA
CBHW060406030726
47497CB00003B/866